I0714316

HEATHER ROSE JONES

THE LANGUAGE OF ROSES

Contents

Acknowledgements...................................ix

CHAPTER ONE: The Briar....................................1

CHAPTER TWO: The Lady in White 2

CHAPTER THREE: The Traveler....................8

CHAPTER FOUR: The Daughter 21

CHAPTER FIVE: The Fée................................33

CHAPTER SIX: The Sacrifice 39

CHAPTER SEVEN: Lady Ice...............................57

CHAPTER EIGHT: The Rose.............................61

CHAPTER NINE: Lord Beast.........................62

CHAPTER TEN: The Guest..........................73

CHAPTER ELEVEN: The Friend....................78

CHAPTER TWELVE: The Jealous Lover...........87

CHAPTER THIRTEEN: The Librarian 93

CHAPTER FOURTEEN: The Thief 105

CHAPTER FIFTEEN: The Confidante 111

CHAPTER SIXTEEN: The Briar................. 117

Contents, continued

CHAPTER SEVENTEEN: The Invisible Ones ... 119

CHAPTER EIGHTEEN: The Watcher 126

CHAPTER NINETEEN: The Visitor 130

CHAPTER TWENTY: The Accuser 139

CHAPTER TWENTY-ONE: The Fugitive.......... 149

CHAPTER TWENTY-TWO: The Guardian 154

CHAPTER TWENTY-THREE: The Prodigal 156

CHAPTER TWENTY-FOUR: The Key............... 166

CHAPTER TWENTY-FIVE: The Betrayer 167

CHAPTER TWENTY-SIX: The Sentinel............ 178

CHAPTER TWENTY-SEVEN: The Thorn.......... 181

CHAPTER TWENTY-EIGHT: The Changeling. 185

CHAPTER TWENTY-NINE: The Sisters 190

CHAPTER THIRTY: The Legend 201

About the Author....................................203

About Queen Of Swords Press....................204

*This story is dedicated to everyone who has
survived a Beast.*

Acknowledgements

I would like to express my deep appreciation for my beta readers: Beth, Irina, Jennifer, Karen, Lauri, Lucy, Maya, Sara, Sharon, and Ursula. You always make my stories better. And most especially for Claudie Arseneault who helped ensure that my aromantic heroine was true to herself.

 THE BRIAR

I DREAM IN THE DARK, longing for brightness and warmth. She is my sun. I feel the heat of her touch, her breath. In the stillness of the dark I speak in roses. When the darkness thins and the walls fade, I call and call. I speak in roses and pour everything I am into that one cry. *Help us!* She is my sun, but the sun is dimming.

CHAPTER TWO

THE LADY IN WHITE

GRACE DU FORTIGNY PICKED her way along the graveled path that led toward the small wrought-iron gate at the back of the barren garden. With an effort that she felt but dared not calculate, she commanded the invisible ones to trail behind her, sweeping the path free of leaves in her wake and dusting across her footprints, erasing the traces of her visit. It left an ache in her bones—an ache like the weight of the curse that hung over the manor of Bettencourt.

Her limbs felt less heavy, less stiff in the morning, and dawn was the only safe time to walk in that corner of the courtyard. There was little chance that Philippe would be watching. Even so, caution led her along a roundabout path, past the bare traces where the hedge maze had once stood and the empty beds that had been a kitchen garden thirty years ago. Past the dry, silent fountain.

She could have asked the invisible ones to tend the gardens. Something might flourish despite the shroud of mist that hid the manor from mortal eyes, but what was the use of that? Philippe provided food for the table with an effortless gesture. Why should she spend her hoarded strength simply for some small bit of sustenance that didn't rely on his pleasure?

She came to the briar that grew beside the gate as if her steps had taken her there by chance. Or as if her only task there was to direct the invisible ones to grease the hinges of the gate. She had neglected that once, long ago. Now it was a habit, out of penance, like the habit of caution in her steps. The rose twisted up from gnarled roots, stretching thorny branches out toward the gaps between the iron bars. Here and there on the brambles, leaves trembled in the breeze seeking the hidden sun. A tiny cluster of buds swelled at the tip of one branch.

Grace reached out to cup stiff fingers around that promise and breathed a kiss of warm air across it. She looked anxiously over her shoulder at the upper windows of the manor. They still showed shuttered against the light. Philippe didn't care for light in the morning even if he woke this early. She turned back to the briar. She had no skill to work with matter. That was Philippe's domain: the transformations, forcing one thing to another. She had only the invisible ones. But here was no need for transformation. The bloom would come on its own.

"What is it?" she asked the rose softly. "What message wakes you?"

The buds swelled between her hands, cracking the petals apart. At first there was a cluster of small white blooms, seeded with red at the center. A tremor fluttered through her heart. *Hopeful news.* A hint of one last chance. She had never entirely lost hope, but it was furled tightly within, like the petals in a swelling bud. Like a river that rushed and tumbled under a skin of ice. She had grown a hard skin long before Peronelle's curse had touched her. Eglantine had coaxed her to dare to bloom that summer, but it was followed by thirty long years back in a habit of stone. Stone kept that bud of hope safe from Philippe's suspicions—not hope for herself, but for what she held most dear.

Grace breathed across the central bud once more and it unfurled, scattering the petals of the smaller blooms across the ground. The flower struggled to open halfway, then just enough more to show the colors within. A broad white simple rose, streaked with purple at its heart. There was no mistaking the sign. "It has been long and long since you sent that message," she said.

She hadn't counted all the failed chances. The last time—that had gone badly indeed. But any change brought…no, she would not name it 'hope' even now. Curiosity. That was the safe thing to call it.

"Thank you," she whispered and brushed her lips across the petals. She could no longer feel their soft touch, but the kiss wasn't for her. In response, a deep crimson blush suffused the bloom before fading to pale shell-pink. "And I, too," she told the rose. "I, too."

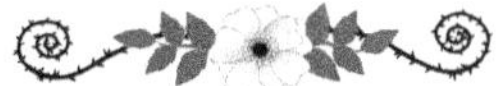

THE INVISIBLE ONES TOLD her when Philippe woke and she sent them to attend on him as much as he would allow. His mood was always better for that attention, even when he raged and cursed at them. The invisible ones didn't mind; they weren't made to mind. Grace considered it worth the ache in her bones to gain that small measure of peace for the day. Other invisible hands made the fires up and laid the board. The food would wait on Philippe's rising, if he deigned to provide it.

She waited until he had filled the pitchers
with wine and waved a careless hand to cover
the platters with food. She waited until she had
eaten enough of her fill that Philippe's whimsical
anger wouldn't leave her hungry until dinner.

"Brother," she said. "We expect a guest
today."

"A guest?" His voice was harsh and suspi-
cious. "A guest?"

He slammed a fist down on the table. The
remains of the meal turned to a smear of mud on
the fine china platters.

Don't flinch. Don't react. Stone and ice. Grace
snapped her fingers and the invisible ones
removed the plates to the kitchen where the rem-
nants of her command would see them washed
and put away.

"A guest, brother. A guest that might be
our salvation if fate is kind." *If you choose to be
kind,* she thought, but those were thoughts that
must never be spoken aloud. Mere kindness
would not be enough for the curse. *Love offered
and returned.* A far distance from simply failing
to terrify. Even that became harder the longer
the curse took hold, but she had to believe it
was possible. "I'll see that a room is prepared.
It might be good to have hospitality ready for
both man and beast."

The word had slipped out before she thought. She'd meant nothing hidden or cruel. That was Philippe's way, not hers. But her brother's glance darted at her suspiciously and his furred muzzle curled in a snarl over yellowed tusks. She never doubted that he would find a way to extract payment.

CHAPTER THREE

THE TRAVELER

NTON LEVESQUE REINED HIS horse in and peered into the deepening mist. Had he taken a wrong turning? The sign posts had been familiar coming up through the rolling vineyards in the valley, but some time after riding into the canopy of the woods the road must have betrayed him. He'd returned this way from Bordeaux every autumn for too many years to count. He wouldn't have missed the way. It was this cursed fog. It had closed in with the twilight and shadows were playing tricks on his memory, as if the trees themselves were luring his mount astray. He urged the horse forward once more. The road dipped down through a shallow pebbled stream and he recognized the way. There should be a woodcutter's hut soon on the left. Perhaps he'd spend the night if it weren't too filthy. If he continued, it would be well past midnight before he saw home. The way would be easier to follow in broad daylight.

A wisp of fog crossed the road bringing a damp chill and the horse shied sideways at something unseen. "Steady! Steady, you brute." When the horse settled again, he stared into the gray emptiness, seeking some threat more solid than weather. The mist thinned slightly to reveal a shadow. What had seemed blank emptiness became a stone wall and the outlines of an arched opening. That didn't belong here. How lost was he? Or...there were stories of a grand manor house somewhere in these woods. A mysterious place that could be found only when its lord chose to be found. The tales told of grand balls and fabulous wealth, but it was said that those who entered the gates came back changed, if they came back at all. Anton shook his head. Nothing but fancies for a winter's evening. Fighting the horse's nervousness, he came close enough for those outlines to become solid.

The wide wrought-iron gates before him were uninviting. The grounds beyond were empty in a way that would be better described as barren than tidy. As far as Anton could see, the yard was deserted. No servants hurried to and fro. Despite that, the property hadn't the look of an abandoned ruin, for the space was cleared of leaves and fallen branches, and what he could see of the manor was in good repair. Another chill breeze shook him. Evening was too far advanced to go farther. One night's delay in returning home meant little. The news he brought could wait.

A sour bitterness rose in his stomach. Always a day late and through no fault of his own. A day late to secure the best contract in Bordeaux, leaving him to scratch and beg for a lesser bargain. If they'd kept the bridge in good repair he would have been there before his rivals. But at least he could spend the night within these deserted stone walls rather than in a drafty woodcutter's hut.

Or was it deserted? He could swear he saw a movement at an upper window. The blur of a face. Perhaps there was hospitality to be found here after all.

Anton swung down from the saddle to find the latch on the gate and pulled it open just enough to bring his horse through. The hinges screamed from long disuse and he cursed as the horse danced back.

"Steady, damn you. Steady. Let's hope there's more than moldy straw for you inside, eh?"

The screeching hinges would have woken the dead, but still no grooms emerged, no footman opened the broad oak doors. Anton circled around to the side yard and found the stables, empty and echoing like the forecourt. But one stall stood ready with clean bedding and sweet hay, with water and grain in buckets. A worried thought crossed Anton's mind. They expected *someone's* return at any moment. The manor's owner? But if there was fodder enough for one, there must be enough for two. And hospitality on the road was a virtue. Once he was inside, he'd let the servants know to make up another stall. Where could they be? Anton grumbled at having to unsaddle the horse himself and brush it out.

Soon he stood again before the iron-bound oak doors of the manor house and lifted the knocker to send an echoing thud into the space beyond. The door must have been unlatched, for it swung open of its own accord at his knock. An entryway led into the darkness beyond but a glow of candlelight invited him to a side parlor. The room was large enough for grandeur but not too large for comfort. A cheering fire blazed on the hearth and a meal was laid on a table beside it, looking for all the world as if the servants that set it out had only just stepped back to the pantry.

Anton called out, "Good evening! Is the master of the house at home?" Clearly he wasn't, though just as clearly they expected him at any moment. That, no doubt, would explain the unlatched door.

"Good evening!" More loudly this time, but still with no response. Not even the sound of distant footsteps.

Anton crossed to warm his hands at the fire and glanced at the array of dishes spread out waiting. How grand it must be to dine so well every night. That was how he had envisioned his life. What he might someday achieve if his luck would only turn and his rivals cease to thwart him at every turn. What would it be like to be not simply respected among his fellows but to be first among them? To host banquets such as this and shower his daughters with gold for their dowries? To run a household that could waste such a meal on the mere chance of their master's return! It would be a pity for the preparations to go to waste, and shame to the manor's owner if hospitality were not shown to a guest.

The dainty pastries heaped on the nearest platter were far too many for any one man to eat. He plucked one up and tasted it. So sweet and delicate. But it needed a bit of wine to wash it down. Something like the crimson contents of the waiting decanter. It would be no trouble for the servants to bring a second glass. He poured a measure and drank. A good vintage and, given his trade, he knew wine. It was uncivilized to enjoy such fine food standing, like a beggar at the door. Anton seated himself at the table and lifted one of the covers—just for curiosity's sake. The rich aroma of the savory ragout enticed him to take just one taste. And then another. The cooking shouldn't go to waste only because the intended diner was absent.

Satisfied and full, Anton took up a candle and went to see to his horse in the stable one last time before sleep. The gray gelding turned its head sleepily to examine him and seemed to want for nothing. It was curious that no second stall had been prepared to serve the master's horse. Had a messenger come to report that he was delayed on the road? No, he'd heard no sounds of any such arrival. And he heard nothing now except the faint hooting of owls out in the woods and the distant muffled bark of a fox.

It was as if some magic curse had snatched up all the inhabitants of the manor at the moment of his arrival...except that his saddle and bridle gleamed with fresh polish. And when he returned to the parlor, not bothering to knock this time, all traces of the meal had been cleared away.

If there had been a chaise there in the parlor, he might have wrapped himself in his greatcoat to sleep on it. But a trail of candles had been lit in sconces leading up the stairs. From the landing he could see a glow from an open door down one corridor. A neat little room, all made up for a weary traveler, with hot water in the pitcher and crisp linen towels, fresh sheets that had known the pass of a warming pan. Even a nightshirt laid out on the bed. That gave him pause, but this was clearly not the bedroom of the master of the house. He could be certain it had been prepared for him, the guest. He washed, undressed, and slipped gratefully between the covers, pulling the bed curtains closed against drafts.

WHEN THE VOICES FIRST entered his consciousness, Anton thought he must be dreaming.

A low, rough voice like the snarl of a beast. "This one is yours, we were agreed."

It was answered with tones as pure and sharp as crystal. "It's no use. Look at him. He'll have a plump cheerful wife back home. Perhaps the next one will be more suitable."

Dreamlike, Anton thought to protest. His wife had left him years past. Neither plump nor cheerful. Suitable? What did—

The bestial voice again. "I doubt the curse cares for such niceties. And we've barely two years left for it to run."

Again, the crystal tones. "A mannerless gray-haired merchant? Perhaps you forget the terms of the curse: love freely given and freely returned. Shall I love him then?"

Anton was full awake and certain this was no dream.

"You've expected me to put on pleasant airs for every wayward chit of a dairymaid that came along." The growling voice sounded more like a petulant child this time.

"Only the pretty ones, give me that."

Menace returned to the low voice. "Bah, I went to all that trouble for dinner and you won't even show your face to give him a try. Now he'll be telling all his neighbors about the magical castle in the woods and we'll never see the end of that."

"There was a time you enjoyed visitors."

"Before that witch Latour's curse. At least for you the curse is no burden, Lady Ice." The taunting voice trailed off into long silence and then came a softer growl. "Better he should never return home."

That chilled Anton to the marrow. He knew that way of thinking. Let a rival see your secrets and there are only two paths to take: bring him all the way in or leave his body on a lonely road.

And whatever this strange household was, he didn't care to be taken in.

The voices had sounded so close they might have been there in the room outside the bed curtains. He could hear no sound of departing footsteps, no creak of doors. There was no way to know what awaited him and sleep was now a stranger. When the first gray sliver of dawn peeked through a crack in the bed hangings, he finally dared to part them and look around.

His clothing of the night before was brushed and pressed and laid out ready. The basin stood empty and the pitcher once again held hot water. Anton didn't stop to wash but hastily dressed and slipped as quietly as he could down the stairs and out to the stable. He hoped to be far away before that monster woke. Though perhaps he had an ally in the house—the crystal-voiced lady?—for his horse was saddled and bridled and waiting for him.

Not the main gate, no. He remembered how it had screamed on its hinges. But there was another, smaller gate piercing the stone wall on the opposite side of the yard. Unlike the main gate, its hinges gleamed with fresh grease. It was wide enough to lead a horse through. Near the gate stood a bramble: a wild unkempt thorn bush that some gardener should have transplanted to a more favorable location—or ripped out entirely, given how scanty the blooms were.

There was only a single rose—a dark pink with a delicate scent that reminded him of a time long ago. Of the curve of a cheek, the glance of an eye. Of the woman who had agreed to be his wife and then deserted him with their youngest newly born. He shook his head to disperse the memory. Why had it come now and here? And why shouldn't he have something pleasant to take away from this place of horrors?

He broke the stem and slipped it into the buttonhole on the lapel of his greatcoat, then stepped toward the gate. When the horse pulled back, snorting, he thought it was only the narrowness of the opening that made it balk. Then a harsh growling voice from behind froze his blood.

"How dare you! *My* rose! No one else is to touch it!"

Anton dreaded to turn but dreaded worse to leave the owner of that voice unseen at his back. It was a grotesque figure, like something out of an old painting: tall and oddly proportioned, with long matted hair and teeth sprouting sideways like tusks. Fingers, gnarled with claw-like nails, grabbed his throat and pulled him so closely he could smell the beast's stinking breath.

"How dare you touch my rose? Your life is forfeit, thief!"

"I…I didn't know. I…oh dear God, be merciful! I was a guest under your roof!"

"A guest who eats my food and sleeps in my bed then sneaks away in the dark of night like a thief to steal my roses."

It would be impolitic, Anton thought absurdly, to point out that it was scarcely the dark of night and that he had heard the beast plotting his death well before any sneaking had occurred. He slipped to his knees as the beast's grasp loosened and held up his arms in supplication. "Forgive me! Don't kill me! I'll pay for the rose. Would you leave my three motherless daughters orphaned entirely?"

"Three daughters?" Another voice chimed in, soft and even.

Glimpsed in the panic of the beast's attack, he had taken the second figure for a marble statue, though he'd seen no statues in the courtyard before. A lady clad all in white stepped forward and reached a finger out to brush the petals of the rose at his collar, then pushed his beseeching hands aside. Her skin was chill and hard, nearly as cold as death. *Fée*, he thought and felt his doom. When fée stepped into the mortal world it meant either rich reward or peril. So much made sense now: the old tales of the enchanted manor, the mysterious dinner of the night before. But why had a fée chosen to reveal herself to *him?*

"Three daughters?" the lady repeated and looked back over her shoulder at the beast. "No doubt you love your daughters very much. Do any of them love you enough to take your place?"

"I…I'm sure that all of them love me enough to make the sacrifice. But what sort of father would I be to ask that of them?" Even as the words left his mouth, he was thinking them over. Cheerful Alys, who had stepped into their mother's place even at the age of seven. Practical Henriette, without whom his business would not have prospered as much as it did. And lovely Louise-Marie, the joy of his life.

"I promise you, she will come to no harm," the lady said in tones that offered no confidence. "She was not the one who stole the rose. Send one of your daughters back to us within three days and your forfeit is paid. Do not think to break the bargain. We will be watching and will fetch you back if need be."

Anton looked from the lady to the other figure. The beast's lip was curled in a snarl, but the shaggy head nodded in agreement.

"Send the prettiest one," the beast growled.

Anton thought of Louise-Marie and his heart sank.

"And here's an earnest for the bargain." The beast crouched down and gathered a handful of gravel from the path, then lifted the flap of one of the gray gelding's saddlebags and let the stones fall within. As they left the beast's hand, they turned to bright gems and lumps of gold.

Anton could only stare in wonder and think it was a conjurer's trick.

"Now go!"

There was no need for more. Anton scrambled to his feet and pulled the reins to drag his horse through the gate, wide-eyed and sidling. Once through, he didn't look back until he had sped far down the road. When he slowed at last to a walk, he could swear he heard the crackle of dry leaves, as if someone walked behind him on the road. But when he dared to turn his head to look, there was no one in sight.

CHAPTER FOUR

THE DAUGHTER

I HANDED THE LAST OF the folded linens to Henriette and said, "There'll be dancing in the market this evening. You two should go." Mending had filled up the morning, but there was no reason for all of us to sit fretting and waiting for another day.

Henriette laid them in the press and tucked a sachet of lavender at one side. "Alys, we should all go. Everyone will ask after you like they did when you missed the Corneilles' ball."

She was looking at me and I braced myself for the old argument as I answered, "With Father not back yet, we must be his presence in the village, as a family. To stand beside the d'Antras and the Montardons as families of importance."

"And Pierre d'Antras will be there," Louise-Marie teased Henriette "It's important to remind *him* that you're still waiting. Will he ask you tonight, do you think?"

"He'll ask me to dance," Henriette said firmly. "Anything else can wait until a suitable time."

They both looked back to me. I reached for the ring of keys that hung from my waist and locked the linen press.

"And there will be guests and travelers there for the harvest fair," Louise-Marie sighed. "There's sure to be someone interesting to catch your eye, Alys."

"There are plenty of interesting people on any day of the year, but someone needs to stay at home." This time I had an excuse to stand firm. More often I gave in. "You know Father will be cross if the house is empty when he arrives."

"It wouldn't be empty," Louise-Marie returned, gesturing at Madame Sauvin, the housekeeper, who was standing by. "The servants—"

"Servants aren't daughters," It was easy for her to dismiss the idea. She was Father's favorite. She wouldn't bear the weight of his displeasure if the household wasn't as he expected. "But you and Henriette should go and dance."

"And watch Jean-Claude dance with every other girl in town," Louise-Marie said with a small pout.

There was no need to remind her that Jean-Claude Corneille's attentions couldn't be too pointed unless a betrothal had been announced.

Henriette's voice turned coaxing. "Alys, you know you'll need to marry someone. No one can offer for us until you're settled. And more to the point, their fathers need to know what will be left for our dowries."

"Jean-Claude says he'd marry me tomorrow if Papa could promise the dowry, and tradition can go hang."

A familiar unease settled in my heart. They were right. Someday I would marry, if only for my sisters' sake. It wasn't fair to make them wait until I was old enough that people were content to leave me an old maid. Someday I would marry, because it was what one did. It wasn't necessary to be in love, like they were. But if you didn't love someone, how did you choose when to say yes? I handed the mending basket to Louise-Marie to put away and answered lightly. "I'm sorry, but I'm not going to fall in love for your convenience."

"You're never going to fall in love at all," Henriette replied. "What are you waiting for?"

What was I waiting for? I'd figured out that Henriette must be in love with Pierre d'Antras, whatever "in love" might mean to her. The two respected each other and looked for the same things from life. They enjoyed spending time together—as much as they were allowed with no betrothal yet. Their understanding had lasted three years so far and would wait on the proper time. Henriette had never been as head-over-heels as Louise-Marie had been with half the boys in town. Jean-Claude was only the latest, and we teased her mercilessly that she'd been waiting for a man with enough names to balance hers. Louise-Marie burned with the sort of love that poets wrote about and sometimes I wondered how much was true and how much was the excitement of the game. I'd never felt anything that could inspire such highs and lows. But…there was something in Henriette's face when she thought of Pierre and when they met in the dance at supper parties or festivals. I sometimes thought that if I ever met someone who could bring that look to my face, I'd be willing to call it love. I guess that was what I was waiting for. Something different from what I felt for my sisters, or for my friends in town, or for my father.

"It's true I don't need to fall in love," I answered at last, "but there needs to be something. Some reason to leave this house and go live with a stranger for the rest of my days.

Until I find that, Father needs me here, looking after you two."

"You wouldn't need to look after us if we were all married," Louise-Marie retorted. Her voice had sharpened from the teasing banter we'd shared while finishing the laundry.

"That's enough," Henriette said. "Take the mending basket upstairs and see to your best gown. I remember you tore the flounce the last time you danced." When Louise-Marie had gone, she said softly, "She isn't really angry, you know."

"I know. Youth is impatient. It will all sort itself out in time." I had faith in that, even if I couldn't see the path. Madame Sauvin was still waiting for instructions and I told her, "See that there's a dinner that keeps well. If our father is late on the road, he'll want a hot meal as soon as he arrives."

"Yes, madame." She gave a brief curtsey and went to talk to Cook.

When had the servants begun addressing me as *madame* rather than *mademoiselle*? It had started so naturally I didn't notice. Perhaps... perhaps it would have been better if Father had remarried. He'd wanted to. There had been that elegant widow visiting the Montardons one summer. Father was so charming, so attentive.

But when his interest became pronounced, the priest took him aside and reminded him that he was not, properly speaking, a widower unless some proof of death could be provided, and the priest wouldn't be party to bigamy.

It was easy to forget that. It had been so long without her. I had a few memories to cling to. The feeling of being held and rocked before the fire and the faint scent of rosewater. There should have been other images, but there was an empty space where they should be. And then there was the memory of reaching down into the cradle and picking up Louise-Marie to say, "Don't cry. I'll be your mother now." Those few memories should be enough. The others didn't even have that much.

As the afternoon started to turn golden, I watched Henriette and Louise-Marie leave in a cloud of laughter and ruffles until they disappeared in the direction of the town square several streets away. I could hear the shrieks of children laughing, muffled when the music started— country dances, not the elegant ballroom sets we'd dance at supper parties. I really did enjoy the bustle of the festivals, where you were as likely to be dancing with the miller's son as with anyone eligible. There wasn't the same awkward presence and attention: men watching your eyes and looking for some sign of encouragement or approval.

I turned my sigh into a rueful smile. It would sort itself out. Just as I was turning back inside, the faint sound of hoofbeats caught my ear. There he was at last, just come into view at the far end of the lane, dusty and tired from the road. I called back into the house, "Jacques! Constance! The master's home!" and heard them rise into a beehive of activity. Everything would be waiting for him. The kitchen had water heated for washing and dinner ready to be served. The parlor was tidy with all the day's chores cleared away. And that was where I welcomed him home, with a curtsey and a respectful kiss.

Father grunted and dropped his saddlebags to the floor, then sank into his favorite chair without a word. I had long practice in gauging his mood. "We're glad to see you safe home, Father."

He looked around. "We? Where are your sisters?"

"They've gone to the harvest festival. You must have heard the music."

He raised his head as if to listen and said, "Fetch them home."

"But Father," I began, "the dancing's only just started."

"Fetch them home."

There was no arguing with him in that mood. I stepped into the next room and stopped Constance in the middle of laying out dishes for supper. "Go fetch my sisters home from the square. Tell them… Tell them our father has news." That must be true enough, no matter what had happened.

"I've sent for them, Father. Let me have Jacques take your bags up to your room."

He placed a foot on one of the loose straps to prevent anyone from moving them and stared at me with a tense and anxious look. There was nothing to be done when he was like that, so I settled myself in the chair opposite him and folded my hands to wait. He didn't like it when I hovered and fussed unless he was of a mind to be fussed over.

If Henriette and Louise-Marie were cross at being called back from the revels, there was no sign of it in their eager welcomes. Louise-Marie threw her arms around our father's neck and kissed him joyously.

"You're home safe! We were so worried. What have you brought us?"

The stage was set at last. Father stood and hefted the saddlebags up to the side table. "Here's what I brought you."

He pulled out a small bundle of papers, tied with a ribbon.

"You made the contract!" Henriette cried out, seizing on it and riffling through the corners of the sheets. Her mouth turned in a faint frown from what she saw there but she said nothing more. She knew what he'd been hoping for. Was that the reason for his mood?

Next he drew out a small bundle tied up in a handkerchief and unknotted the corners to release a spill of gold and jewels across the table. Where had that come from? And why would it leave him anxious and fretting?

"Oh, Father!" Louise-Marie breathed. "That's more than twice our dowries! Jean-Claude will be so happy." She ran her fingers through the treasure, marveling at the weight of the gold.

Last, he pulled out a flower. A pink rose that looked scarcely the worse for wear for having been carried in a saddlebag. It, too, was laid on the table. In puzzlement, I picked it up and raised it to breathe in the scent. I'd always loved roses. "It's beautiful, Father." I was uncertain what else to say.

"Do you know what that rose has cost me?" He had sat again and was staring down at clenched hands.

The flower burned in my fingers like a hot coal and my sisters were staring at me. "Father, I don't understand. A rose?"

He looked up and repeated, "Do you know what that rose has cost me?"

And then he told a tale as wondrous as any in a book: a strange deserted mansion, a mysterious dinner, whispers in the night, and then, just as he thought he would escape safely, the rose and the hideous monster, the threat and the bargain with the fée.

There was a long silence when the story came to an end. I had been staring at the flower to avoid meeting Father's eyes. When I looked up, my sisters were watching me closely. Did they all see it as a sign that I had picked up the flower? Each of them had seized on what was closest to their hearts. The rose had meant nothing special. It was only what they'd left to me. And there was the answer. They had dreams and plans and lovers waiting for them, and I—I had them. I had spent all my life caring for them and protecting them and doing what I could to make all our lives easy and pleasant. Now there was Father, staring at me holding the rose, his face filled with horror and regret. And there were Henriette and Louise-Marie, looking terrified. And I could solve it all with a word.

Thinking about the matter longer wouldn't change what I knew I must do. If one of the three of us must take Father's place, who was a better choice? Henriette couldn't be spared if the business was to thrive, and Louise-Marie had so much before her. She'd won the heart of the son of the most powerful man in town, and now she had the gold to win his father's heart as well. When we had all been younger, my sisters had needed my care, but now? Now I could still do this thing for them.

"I'll go," I said quietly.

At first, Father looked as if he hadn't quite heard, then he sagged back against the cushions of the chair.

"Father, I'll take your place." I tucked the rose into the edge of my fichu and left the room quickly to see that dinner was laid in the next room. And so I didn't need to see the look of relief in all their faces. No, it was the right decision. We all knew that.

I laid the rose beside my pillow that night. It wouldn't last much longer and perhaps I could enjoy the scent before it faded. Such a little thing for so great a cost.

Perhaps it was no wonder that my dreams were filled with strange visions. I saw two women, one carved from wood and one from stone, and there was a wolf prowling to and fro at their feet. The scent of roses was woven through it all.

The roses, at least, could be explained. When I woke, it still lay there beside my pillow, as fresh as it might have been when first plucked. I lifted it to my face once more. Yesterday, I thought it had been a pure soft pink, like the inside of a shell from far-off islands that Father once brought home. But now I saw that it was brushed inside with red.

CHAPTER FIVE

THE FÉE

A H, PERONELLE! YOU ARE patient now. Patient enough to stand outside the gates of Bettencourt for days to see what might befall. You were not so patient when you were…but no, you were not young then. It has been very long since you were young, hasn't it? The fée are young only once and old for a very long time. But one may be impatient at any age. Do you remember when you were young, Peronelle? Do you remember the glittering halls of Tourdespine and the guests your parents hosted for balls and hunting parties? How they would ride out to slip between the worlds and tease those in mortal lands. Do you remember learning to walk the worlds for yourself? How to draw glamour after you to hide the truth from mortal eyes? Do you remember how it felt to be new come into your power and uncertain? To make mistakes? But one may be foolish and make mistakes at any age. Isn't that so, Peronelle?

There was no need for patience then. You were eager to seize the world in your hands, to touch each seed of promise and feel it grow beneath your fingers. Green and growing things were your gift. You knew how the world worked in the certainty of your power. Your parents left Tourdespine in your keeping and went to walk the worlds again. That is what fée do when they see their children grown and settled. Your fame and power increased. You were certain of the shape your life would take. The world had rules and you knew them as you knew the stone walls of Tourdespine.

You knew with a certainty beyond doubt where your path would lead. Just as you had thrived in your parents' affection, you knew what love to expect from a husband, from a child. But the world has plans of its own.

She was the child of your heart, wasn't she, Peronelle? You hadn't yet thought to contemplate a child of your body. No man, whether of the fée or of mortal lands, had yet sparked the fire you surely knew would someday come. You were patient. But oh! They brought her to you, a shy and weeping child, hoping that you could lift her curse. It was no curse, was it? Simply a gift gone awry. With every sob and hiccup, flowers and jewels fell from her dainty lips: violets and asphodel, pearls and rubies, gillyflowers and columbine, sharp brilliant diamonds and cruel sweet thorny roses, tearing her lips and throat until she screamed. And you, Peronelle, you took her in your arms and kissed her bleeding lips, tasting of rose and violet, and promised to teach her how to shape her gift. The mouth was for words and kisses, you said. Sorcery belonged to the hands.

She struck you to the heart, didn't she, Peronelle? Her parents poured out their gratitude and relief and promised you anything you desired. And you found you desired a daughter: a child to teach the language of green and growing things. What could they do? They left her to your care. That's what fée do, isn't it? They leave.

There was no need for patience then, Peronelle. She was the daughter of your heart, the student of your dreams. She grew and learned and blossomed. She was the darling of your guests, the joy of every ball, plucking flowers and bright jewels out of the air and speaking in the language of roses. She drew the eye of the du Fortignys, the masters of Bettencourt, and they begged, "Let her come to visit our son Philippe, now he is grown to mastery. It is time for us to walk the worlds and he needs a wife to steady him, an alliance to build his influence. Let her come to see if they suit."

You weren't ready to let her go yet, were you, Peronelle? She was your darling and your child.

No other love had come to claim your heart—
no one who fit the shape you'd saved for him in
your life. But she laughed and said though she
had no mind to wed just yet, she wished to visit
Bettencourt.

You brought her there in pomp and celebra-
tion. And because you didn't care to return alone
to Tourdespine, you went to travel distant lands
and play with mortal lives. You promised to
return. A year and a day, and then if she wished
there would be a wedding such as had not been
seen in a mortal lifetime. The world had rules
and you would follow them.

A year and a day. You never doubted you would
see her again, did you, Peronelle? You returned
and she was gone with all her retinue and no one
would say a word. You raged and you warned and
you pleaded and no one would tell you where she
had gone or why, not cruel Philippe nor silent
Grace. You cursed yourself that you hadn't seen
their hearts before. So many things you didn't see.
The world had rules and when they stepped outside the bounds, they drew their own doom. You
cursed yourself with words, but you cursed them
with ancient power. You cursed them as you saw
them: the cruel beast and the silent stone. Ah yes,
so many things you didn't see.

You had no patience then, Peronelle. You
meant the curse as a punishment, as a threat to

loosen their tongues. Surely, they must know where your child had gone, what had sent her fleeing from Bettencourt. But Philippe only laughed. He knew the laws that bound you and that every curse must have its key. You made that key as cruel as his laughter. And then you left to search for your daughter through every world you knew.

Half a dozen years you sought her, locked in anguish and despair, and never found a trace. Then half a dozen more, wandering alone, seeking solace, as Tourdespine fell to empty ruin.

You thought a mortal interlude might heal your heart. You thought him a simple, uncomplicated man. He adored you with the love you'd always thought to win. He promised you anything your heart desired and you thought to fill your empty arms with mortal children to erase that other loss. But mortal men cannot be trusted with a heart. You discovered that, didn't you, Peronelle? You married him with vows and words within a church that trapped you in his world and thought you could be content.

He promised you everything your heart desired, but he lied. That's what mortals do: they lie. His selfish faithlessness set you free. You, but not your mortal children—they were too young to make that choice. They had been signed with holy water and their blood still bound them to that world. You could not take them and you would not stay. And so you left. That's what fée do, isn't it, Peronelle?

Oh, but Peronelle, now you have learned patience. If you have not been granted the love you were promised, you can still punish those who broke your heart. You set your spies at Bettencourt, and every time they raise the glamour to let the mortal world in, you know. Nothing comes of it. You can't pierce their defenses but you know that much. If the du Fortignys had succeeded in enticing an innocent within those walls, if one of them had known and offered true love, you would have felt it when the chains broke. Their glamour is fraying now as the curse comes near fulfillment. You know that calendar written in your bones. Three days and three and thirty years. A span to conjure with. Nearly the whole of it is accomplished. If those two succeed at the last, you will be there to witness. And if they fail, you will witness that as well and your heart will find its rest.

Now, the gates have opened once more, both those of iron and those of sorcery, and you wait outside to see what may befall. You are patient now.

CHAPTER SIX

The Sacrifice

I SET OUT THE VERY next day. I gave the keys to the household into Madame Sauvin's keeping and kissed them all goodbye. Henriette and Louise-Marie clung to me weeping and I dried their cheeks one last time and shooed them back into the house saying, "Let me remember you laughing and happy. Let me take that with me, not tears."

What would be the use of lingering? It would only have given me more time to fear, more time for my sisters to mourn, more time for my father to refuse to meet my eyes. There was little enough to pack. How could I know what garments I might need? *I promise you she will come to no harm.* That's what Father had said the Pale Lady told him. But what could such a promise mean to a lord and lady of the fée? What use would they have for me?

I put on a good warm traveling dress, with skirts wide enough for riding, and a woolen cloak. In the saddlebags I rolled up a change or two of linens with such necessities as a woman might need. And on top of them I laid the rose. There was no question in my mind but that I would bring the rose—the symbol of my sacrifice. It would fade soon enough, but the scent that lingered in the dry petals might comfort me.

I rode out through the gates by noon, with neither groom nor maid—*let her come alone,* they had said—taking only Father's gray gelding and the promise that the horse would know its way. I knew the beginning of the road, the one Father always took. I had never been so far from home and never alone. But when the road forked, or the track faded, the horse would turn its head as if from a pull on the reins. Sometimes, if I listened past the horse's hoofbeats, I could hear other footsteps pacing beside me. The memory of my dream came back and I half expected to see the form of a wolf shadowing my path.

Dusk was falling when I passed a small hut a stone's throw from the road and thought to shelter for the night, for there was no hint of how much farther the mysterious manor might be. No one answered my call, and I had to dismount to fight the reins against my unseen guides who tried to force the gelding onward. I didn't see the woman in the long dark cloak when she stepped out from the shadows until she called to me, "Are you come to Bettencourt?"

Was this the Pale Lady of Father's tale? No, he'd said that one had the look of a marble statue. This one had warm and rosy flesh.

"I—I don't know," I stammered. "That is, I neither know whether Bettencourt is my goal or if I've come to it."

"Girls who enter Bettencourt are lost," the woman said.

"How do you know? Who are you?"

The woman didn't come closer, but pushed her hood back so I could see her face. It was a pleasant face, neither old nor young, with hair that might have been mousy brown or beginning to be touched with gray. Her eyes were hard and full of sorrow.

"My dearest one entered those gates," she said, "and was never seen again."

The courage I had brought with me drained away, leaving me hollow. I filled that hollow with thoughts of Henriette and Louise-Marie.

"What happened to her?" I asked. I envisioned an unmarked grave in a corner of a garden, or a locked chamber in the cellar.

"I don't know." Her voice was bleak. "I have no power to see within someone else's magic."

"Magic," I echoed. I had known there would be magic. Everything in Father's story spoke of it. But...*someone else's magic.* "Do you have magic of your own?" Who but a fée would linger here in the middle of an empty wood?

She nodded. "I have my own. Not the sort that transforms, but the sort that reveals things as they truly are. And what are you? Why are you here?"

Following hard on the heels of her claim, there was menace in her words. What was I, truly? What should I reveal? I seized on the second question.

"My father offended the lord of...of Bettencourt, I suppose, if that's where I'm going. I've come to pay his forfeit."

"Then your fate is chosen already."

Now the stranger did come forward and took my chin in her hand to examine my face with a curious, troubled gaze.

"You have come out of love," she said at last. "Perhaps..." Then her voice hardened. "You will fail as all the others have. But it is not much farther, if they choose to open the gates to you." With that, she turned and disappeared under the trees once more.

I puzzled over her words. Of course, I'd come out of love, as well as duty and the relentless logic of an impossible choice. I bit my lip and thought of home, a bare day's journey behind me. But what did she mean that I would fail?

There was no mounting block to hand, but the lady had said it wasn't far, so I continued down the road, leading the horse behind me. And then, between one moment and the next, I saw a wide black iron gate across my path, with stone walls leading off into the growing dark on either side. This must be the end of my journey. I grasped the horse's reins more tightly and stepped forward to push the gate open. It screamed on its hinges like a lost soul. As I passed through, something caught at me—a cobweb, a filmy veil—but it dissolved into no more than an icy mist.

IT WAS JUST AS Father had described. The light of a lantern led me to the stable where a stall was prepared. I wondered if I should leave the horse to the care of the unseen servants, but that would be poor recompense for carrying me if they didn't come, so I struggled with the unfamiliar tasks of removing saddle and bridle, then took the bundle with my few possessions from the saddle bag and went to find the door.

There was no sign of my hosts in the hall. A trail of candles led the way past darkened rooms, up a sweeping staircase, and to a chamber that might have been the same one Father occupied. The bed with its rich hangings stood just as he'd described, with a basin and steaming water standing by and all things needful for a weary traveler. And then, when hunger and curiosity had beaten back the fear, I descended the stairs once more and saw light shining from a doorway that had been dark before. I could see a table laid for dining, with candles blazing and the flickering of a cheery fire. A table laid for three. That was different from Father's story.

If there had been only a single setting, I think I would have sat to dine and pushed away the thought of meeting my hosts. But they meant to join me, that was clear, and courtesy forbade. So I waited. And waited. With every minute that passed, my heart beat more frantically. My hands grew cold and I turned to the fire to warm them.

"Welcome to Bettencourt."

The voice rose behind me, smooth and even. It seemed to suck the heat of the fire out of the room.

I turned quickly, betraying my fear. It was not the speaker that drew my eyes, but the man behind her. Man? I scarcely knew whether to give him that name. Father's words came back to me. *Not man, but beast. Some demon out of hell.* But neither did that seem to fit. He looked hunched and twisted, as if the limbs beneath his clothes had a different shape than a man's, yet he held himself with an air of pride and confidence that suited his noble garments. The hands that emerged from lace-bedecked cuffs were like a man's except for the thick claw-like nails that tipped each finger. The head had the shape of a man's if one made allowance for how his mouth thrust forward like the muzzle of a bear or a wolf, and long, yellowed teeth showed when he made as if to smile. Yet the smile seemed warm and welcoming—more welcome than a common girl like me should expect in a grand and noble house such as this.

I couldn't help taking a step back toward the hearth as the creature came toward me and held out one...paw? Hand? This closely I could see that a fine pale fur covered all his skin. His voice sounded like the rumble of an enormous cat's purr.

"Let me welcome you to my home. You may call me Lord Bête, and this is my sister, Lady Glace."

Not knowing what to do, I raised my hand to his and dipped in a curtsey, treating it as a gesture of welcome. His claws scraped my palm as he raised my fingers to his lips and I shivered. It took all the courage I had not to shrink away, and all the manners I could summon to hide that effort.

"L…Lord Beast and Lady Ice?" I said hesitantly.

The woman nodded slowly, returning the most formal of welcomes. I could see why Father had known her for fée. Her skin was the smooth, pale hardness of polished stone and her gaze held a distance that suggested disdain for mortal things. She was dressed all in white.

"My brother makes a little joke to put you at ease," she said. "I am Grace du Fortigny, and this is my brother Philippe du Fortigny, the master of this place. And you are one of the daughters of Monsieur Levesque."

"A…Alys," I replied, recovering my hand from Lord Philippe's grasp.

"A little joke to put you at ease," Lady Grace repeated, "lest you think it discourteous to speak of the curse we are under. We hope you will find us as pleasant company as you are to be to us."

Company. Was that to be the name of my captivity? It was a word that didn't admit of the threat of violence and vengeance that brought me here. The mere presence of the beast was enough reminder of that.

It was the strangest meal I had ever been served, or ever hoped to. I was placed at one side of the table, with Lady Grace and Lord Philippe facing each other at either end. The table was laden with roasted meats tucked in pastry and dainty croquettes and jellies and forcemeats. There were no servants to be seen, but every time I turned my head or blinked my eyes, the dishes on the table would change: the covers removed, wine filling the glasses. The first time it happened, I couldn't check a little gasp.

Lord Philippe gave a bark of laughter and I shrank into myself from embarrassment, but I think he couldn't help how his voice sounded any more than he could help the shape of his limbs. Then he smiled at me with a more friendly air and raised his glass in my direction as an apology.

Lady Grace said evenly, "You needn't fear the invisible ones. They do my bidding. You have only to speak a wish aloud and as long as we permit it, it will be done."

I looked around, expecting to find some sign of those silent hands, despite the name she had given them. "Are they…people?" I've heard a saying that the best servants are invisible, but to curse them to being utterly unseen seemed cruel.

"They're bits of Lady Ice's sorcery," Lord Philippe said, "that she *pinches* off—" he made a gesture in the air "—and sends to do her bidding."

Why did he call her that? A joke, she'd said, but I'd learned to read feelings beneath people's words. He baited her while she was all courtesy to him.

"Are you a sorcerer as well?" I asked. I wondered if the question were impudent, but he was the one to have spoken of magic first. And if Lady Grace were his sister, then he too must be fée, whatever the curse had made him.

Lord Philippe seemed not to have heard my question. "Is the dinner to your liking? You've barely touched a bite. What is your favorite dish? Anything at all!"

"I…" Would he send the invisible ones off to the kitchen to prepare it on the spot? Was this an offer of hospitality or a test of my good sense? I tried to think of something that wouldn't be too much trouble or delay the meal too far. What might they have on hand that I could ask for? "On a cold autumn evening like this," I began hesitantly, "I'm always fond of a good soup with sausages."

Philippe's muzzle wrinkled into an expression I couldn't read, except to guess that my answer had been wrong. What should I have said instead?

"Soup with sausages," he said and waved his hand over the table. The pastries and croquettes and dainty dishes vanished and in their place, before each of us, stood a bowl steaming with sliced cabbage and onions and rich fat chunks of sausage. "Our guest has requested that we dine on soup with sausages."

I cringed inside, but how could I have known that he could conjure food from the empty air? I poised my spoon above the bowl before remembering the stories of fairy gold that would wither into dry leaves in the morning and thinking of the gold and jewels Father had brought home for Louise-Marie's dowry. But Lord Philippe's eyes watched me closely and I brought a spoonful to my lips, blew it to coolness, and sipped. It was the most delicious soup I had ever tasted.

My surprise must have shown on my face for Lady Grace explained, "My brother cannot conjure substance from nothingness, but only transform one thing to another. The food in front of you is as real and true as what was there before." She lifted her own spoon and addressed the soup delicately but efficiently, as if she thought it might change again before her eyes.

Lady Grace's answer had been very precise. *As real as what was there before.* But it tasted like good pork broth and I pushed aside the question of what the roast meats and pastries had been before they came from the kitchen.

"You see," Lord Philippe said. "As with the invisible ones, you have only to tell me what you want and it will be provided."

We ate for a while in silence and I made lists in my mind of what I might ask for the next time we dined so that I wouldn't disappoint him again.

Lady Grace began conversing lightly of inconsequential matters—I scarcely knew what. There was nothing we could speak of in common, not the small doings of neighbors nor great news of wars or royal marriages. "We have been out of the world for some time," she said, as one might mention having been away for a visit. "You will need to tell us how things get on among—" She hesitated and I wondered what she meant to say, but she only continued, "among the people of this land."

I nodded and tried to think what I might have to say to a lord and lady that would entertain them.

"Have you been traveling, then?"

Lord Philippe grinned. It seemed a friendly grin, but I quickly looked away from the unquieting sight of his long teeth. "Bettencourt has existed for an age and more, but the gates are only open where and when it pleases me. Ask an old woman in your village and she might remember nights of dancing and pleasure in my father's day. We are found when we choose to be."

There was to be no second course, it seemed. When we had all finished our soup, Lord Philippe stood and extended his hand to me proclaiming, "Now we will dance."

"I am not dressed for dancing, my lord," I said quietly. I still wore the traveling dress I had arrived in and now I wondered what I would do for clothing as it seemed that I wasn't to be beheaded or eaten.

Lord Philippe frowned impatiently—I was quickly learning to read his reactions through the mask of his beast-face. "Have I not said that you have only to tell me what you want?"

He gestured at me from neck to toes and my plain dress was gone, replaced by a gown of satin and lace, looped over panniers and spangled with silver passementerie. I shivered, thinking that if he could conjure clothing so easily he could conjure its lack. When I feared for my life, I hadn't thought to fear more ordinary things.

"Does it please you?" he asked, still holding his hand out to take mine.

"It's a beautiful gown," I said and rose from the table, allowing myself to be led into the open space before the hearth.

Lord Philippe glanced over at his sister and commanded, "Music!"

Though Lady Grace made no movement, in the corner of the room, a harpsichord began playing.

We moved through a stately, old-fashioned dance that I scarcely remembered. His hand guided me through the measures when I was uncertain. Each time we turned, I could see Lady Grace sitting still and silent at the table watching us.

The music ceased and our steps came to a stop. As we rose from our reverence, I found both hands trapped in Lord Philippe's grasp. The moment stretched out, with his eyes fastened on mine and our faces so close that I could feel his hot breath stirring my hair. Just when I thought I must scream to bring some end to it, he said in a low growling voice, "Alys, can you love me? Will you marry me?"

Marry him! If I had tried for a hundred years to imagine what this evening might bring, I would never have guessed it would be that! I could only stand and stare and wish myself anywhere but in that gilded parlor, quaking at the thought of what my refusal would bring.

It wasn't that I had never received a proposal of marriage before, though I'd never told my sisters and certainly not Father. François Montardon led me aside, one quiet summer evening after a supper party, and held my hand to his heart and asked, "Do you think you could ever love me enough to marry me?"

We had been friends since we were children. He was a good man. He searched my face so earnestly and I thought perhaps… I wanted to be kind, so I said, "If you wish to marry me, I will. But if you need me to love you, then I think we would be unhappy."

He begged me to consider carefully. But what was there to consider? I could only speak what I felt—I owed him that. Within the year, his heart had turned to another. And when I saw them together, laughing at some private joke or touching each other's hands in passing for no reason at all, I knew I'd given him the right answer.

And now this stranger, this beast, stood before me and asked, *Can you love me? Will you marry me?* And I trembled like a rabbit trapped by the hounds. He must be mocking me. Teasing me with stories about how the prince marries a goose girl.

I felt a chill like ice in my veins and realized that Lady Grace had grasped my wrist and gently pulled my hands free of Lord Philippe's.

"That is enough for one evening, I think."

She began to lead me away but when I looked back, Lord Philippe leaned slumped against the mantlepiece and was gazing at the fire, as if he had suffered a great disappointment.

"You needn't fear to answer truly," Grace said as she preceded me up the stairs with slow and stately tread. "Go take your rest and remember: if there's anything you want, ask the invisible ones."

She left me at the door to my chamber. So many things I wanted to ask, but I only nodded and closed the door behind me. In that chill, dim silence I began to shake until my limbs could no longer hold me. I fell to the floor trying not to weep. When I thought I could bear no more, I felt a gentle touch on my cheek, smearing away a tear. I jerked away but even in the dim firelight I knew there was no one in the room with me. *The invisible ones.* Hesitantly, I asked, "Could you light the candles, if you please?"

Light flared from sconces on the walls.

"If you please, could you make up the fire?"

The logs on the hearth shifted, rousing into a bright blaze.

I reached up for the bedpost and pulled myself to my feet. A ruffled nightdress lay across the bed. "Could you—" What were the invisible ones, I wondered. Were they spirits? Were they male and female? "Could you help me undress?"

Unseen hands plucked at the pins and laces of my gown. I felt it loosen about me and fall to pool on the floor. The panniers folded themselves in a heap and the corset laces slipped out of their holes. I stepped out of the shoes and quickly traded my chemise for the nightdress. When I turned to the dressing table, there was a row of combs and brushes that had not been there before. Beside them lay the rose—or one as like to it as its twin, still fresh and bright.

I picked it up and held it to my cheek. "Oh, rose! What am I doing here? What does he want from me?" The invisible ones plucked the pins from my hair and I felt it tumble free, but I was too weary to brush and plait it before slipping between the covers of the bed.

Remembering the story Father had told about the voices in the night, the last thing I asked was, "If you please, could you—if it is permitted to ask—could you lock the door?"

I held my breath and waited until I heard the scratch of a key in the lock. It was a little thing, and no doubt the du Fortignys could easily command their invisible servants to unlock it again if they chose. But I was able to sleep.

CHAPTER SEVEN

LADY ICE

GRACE RETURNED TO THE parlor, feeling the stirrings of the invisible ones as they attended to their guest. Philippe paced back and forth before the fire. The table had been cleared of the remains of dinner and her bones ached with the accumulated weight of the tasks. Did Philippe's sorcery also wear more on him the deeper the curse took hold? He never gave an outward sign, but neither did she.

He turned as she came in and said, "Well, my Lady Glace, will she be our salvation, do you think? Does she have it in her to love me?"

Lady Glace. That had been the first lesson Philippe had taught her. The earliest memory she had, back when her childish tongue had stumbled over the sounds of her own name. Philippe would tease her, tormenting her to tears with rhymes and cruel tricks. *Ice is nice my Lady Glace,* and then her coif would turn to snow. Their nurse would laugh at them, then dry her eyes, saying it was only a joke. But Nurse had already felt the bite of Philippe's tricks and she found reasons not to punish him.

Appealing to their parents was no more use than praying to the mortals' God. *A young lady doesn't throw tantrums. A young lady is quiet and polite.* And from their father, *You must respect your elder brother, for some day he will be lord here.* So she had learned to hold her tongue and keep her tears inside until the gibing nickname was little more than a habit for Philippe and he'd almost forgotten it was meant to wound. By then, other lessons had pushed that one aside. Philippe grew into his sorcery more quickly, always three steps ahead of her own. She soon learned the most important lesson: never betray what she most cared about. Never give Philippe a hostage to her heart.

And so she locked away her pity and hope for Alys Levesque and smoothed her voice of any trace of criticism. "She seems a sweet and biddable girl. I think, once she is allowed time to become comfortable—"

"Isn't this comfort enough?" Philippe asked, waving his hand to take in the manor. "A banquet at every meal. The finest of furnishings. Elegant clothing."

"The confidence that you don't intend to eat her," Grace added lightly, trying to make it sound an extension of his own thoughts. "We threatened her father with death. How could she guess you have more tender feelings towards her?"

Philippe grunted. "Time, then. How much time does it take to fall in love?"

He gave her a sly, sideways glance that Grace pretended not to see as she took her leave. He would know better than she did. She had only fallen the once. But in the years before Peronelle's curse, he had courted a succession of possible brides. He fell easily, and women found him charming, but such feelings never aligned. He rejected this one because she was too eager. That one had seen through his attentiveness and made excuses. A third wielded sorcery that looked fair to overmaster his own and he couldn't bear a rival. Only once had his interest been caught and held to the point of proposal. Once, he had put all his efforts into wooing and pursuit. There are few things more attractive than that which you cannot have. And Philippe was accustomed to having anything he wanted.

Perhaps Alys Levesque, too, would succeed by requiring pursuit. Her shy reluctance might coax a genuine interest from Philippe. If his heart could be turned to her, there was no reason to doubt that hers could follow. And then there was hope that both their curses would be broken. Once his heart was captured by a new love, surely he would let the old one go. Perhaps she could give Alys a hint…but no. She was too acquainted with Peronelle's mind. *Love freely returned*—that was the key. How could Alys give something freely if she knew what depended on it?

Grace paused at the base of the stairs aching for the repose that lay above. But first this. With every day, the climb became harder and more painful. She would not let it show. Would not betray how close the curse felt to its final triumph. With a straight back and slow, smooth movements that spoke of nothing but pride and dignity, she set her foot on the stair.

CHAPTER EIGHT

THE ROSE

CAN YOU HEAR ME, little one? Can you understand? I have forgotten how to speak in words. I cried so long into the empty darkness with no one to hear except my love. Has my voice grown louder now? I hear you whispering to me. I walk through your dreams but you don't answer me.

How long did I fight through the silence after he worked his will on me? A year? Two? The same span as my childish tongue was tangled? In those days I spoke in diamonds and daffodils and they stopped my mouth. But now I find my voice again in roses.

Do you understand the language of roses, little one? There are secrets I need to tell you. We need you, she and I, but she is too afraid to speak. And I? I can only speak in roses.

CHAPTER NINE

Lord Beast

I THINK I DREAMED THAT night of my mother—of what I could remember of her: the scent of rosewater flowing through my mind and the slow rocking of arms holding me. My sisters were there too. I could feel their presence though I couldn't see them. And then came dawn, and the sick, sinking knowledge that I was alone to face…I didn't know what I faced and that was what ran under my skin like prickling fire. I would never sleep easy again.

The rose lay beside my pillow. I thought I'd left it on the dressing table, but I must have reached for it in the night. It must be fading now at last, for the petals had turned from pink to yellow and the bright red at the heart to pink, but they were still supple and not dry at all. "I'm sorry," I whispered to it as I hid it underneath my pillow. Would the unseen servants let it be or consider it rubbish to be taken away?

I paced the room, listening for sounds of my hosts stirring elsewhere in the manor and wishing I could stay shut in forever. I asked the invisible ones for warm water to wash, but when I asked them for a bit of bread to break my fast, nothing appeared on the little table by the window. So it would be hunger that would drive me downstairs in time.

I had no clothing but the gown that Lord Philippe had provided for the dancing. Not even my old traveling dress—God alone knew where it had disappeared to! Or had its substance been transformed? What had last night's dinner been before being touched by Lord Philippe's sorcery? It seemed better not to ask the question. When I heard the creaking of floors and the thud of footsteps, I asked the unseen servants to dress me in the satin gown. The sun had moved toward noon—that is, the light suggested that hour. When I peered out the window, I could see nothing beyond the boundaries of the manor's walls and gates. Nothing but a gray mist.

It was unsettling to be dressed by unseen hands: to raise my arms and feel the corset wrap around me and tighten, to reach back and find the sleeves awaiting my hands. More unsettling than seeing nothing was that there was nothing not to see. Every movement was just beyond my vision. Hands worked when I turned my head or blinked. There was always a sense that if I turned unexpectedly, I would catch them at their work. If I closed my eyes…no, that was too frightening. When I closed my eyes, I thought I could *see* those invisible hands. Finally, I stood at the glass and could find no further excuse for delay.

Only Lord Philippe was in the parlor when I entered. I had thought there might be a breakfast room. I'd never been in a house grander than the Corneilles' before and they would never think of spending all their lives in a single room, but as I passed other doorways, they were dark. Something in their shadows made my gaze slip away and I trembled at the thought of exploring those spaces. It made the manor feel both smaller and immense.

There were tea and pastries on the table. Philippe rose with those ungainly limbs and led me to the chair I'd occupied the night before. He leaned over me as I settled myself.

"Did you sleep well, Alys? Is the food to your liking? Is there anything you desire?"

I don't think he could have heard my whispered answer, but it didn't seem to matter. Lord Philippe took his own chair and watched me closely as I ate and drank. The hunger that had driven me from my chamber ebbed away. I set down my cup.

"My lord?"

"Yes, Alys?"

"You said that I might ask for clothing. I came here in such a rush that I had no thought what to pack…"

"Yes, of course," he said eagerly. "What would you like?"

I didn't want to sound greedy. A very few things would do. "This gown is lovely for dancing," I said. "But perhaps a plain one for everyday? One in which I might—" What *would* I be doing every day? Not directing the servants or supervising the mending or going to the market or any of the many other things that had occupied my time in Father's house. "One in which I might walk in the gardens. Or see to my father's horse. Something less grand for mornings."

Lord Philippe's brows narrowed but I was only beginning to learn to read his moods. Was it a frown or only thoughtfulness? "The horse has been sent home," he said. Then he gestured at my clothing as he had the night before and I found myself dressed in a dark woolen smock such as a shepherdess might wear. Perhaps he had no idea of the fashions of townswomen.

"I had thought—" Oh, now I did feel like I stepped too far! "I would not want to bother my lord each time I wish to change my garments…"

"I have told you," he said with a touch of impatience, "that you have only to request what you want."

"But if she wants to put on different garments when she rises at dawn, she would find it rude to disturb your rest."

I hadn't seen Lady Grace enter, so careful and quiet were her steps. I nodded in grateful agreement.

Lord Philippe's muzzle twitched again and he rose. "As you wish."

With his words, a heap of clothing appeared on the floor beside him: folds of satin and brocade, delicate swaths of lace, the sparkle of gold and silver embroidery. Nothing of a more practical nature, but perhaps he would allow me to keep the one I now wore as long as I dressed more finely for the evening.

"Now since you wish to go walking in the garden—though what there is to see, I couldn't say—take these things up to your chamber and then come to join me."

LORD PHILIPPE WAS RIGHT to say that the gardens held nothing much to see. There was a fountain filled with green-scummed water, set in the middle of a maze of graveled paths that skirted beds empty even of weeds. And though I wanted to see flowers, I wanted even more a chance to be alone for a time. That was not to be, as Philippe took my arm and led me through the barren grounds, carefully attentive and speaking of this and that. There was no sign of vegetation except for the dry leaves that blew over the walls—that and a twisted briar at the edge of the yard, near a small arched gate in the stone wall. I gave a little gasp when I saw it, recognizing that it must be the rose that had been Father's downfall. I would have walked on past, but Lord Philippe had heard me and turned our steps to go nearer.

"Do you like my rose?" he asked and broke the flower from its stem to hold it to my nose.

I could see a deep gold at the base of the petals and it smelled faintly of licorice or basil. How could one bush bear so many colors? Perhaps some clever gardener had grafted it together from many parts. I thought Philippe was offering the flower as a gift, but when I went to take it, he snatched it back and slipped it into the buttonhole at his collar.

"It's very beautiful," I offered.

Philippe sucked at his finger where a thorn had pierced it. "Beautiful and treacherous." He looked down at me, "Women so often are. But not you. I can tell that you're different from most women: gentle, generous. You can see truly into the heart of things." He made as if to stroke the edge of my chin, then pulled his hand away. "Ah, but I presume too much. Not even one as generous as you could find it in your heart to see past this." He gestured at his face, then made as if to tear at it with his claws and sharply turned away.

"Don't! Please don't!" I cried and I caught at his wrist. Then I let him take my arm again to lead me away from the briar beside the gate.

WHEN EVENING CAME, I chose my favorite of the gowns Philippe had created for me and allowed the unseen servants to dress my hair as if I were a lady of the court. This time, when I entered the parlor and found my two hosts waiting in their accustomed places at the table, there was no food filling the dishes, only piles of dry leaves and twigs.

"How shall we dine tonight?" Philippe asked as I sat. My chair was slipped in beneath me by invisible hands.

I warmed to the game this time, trying not to think about the leaves, and suggested a list of dishes that I recalled from the banquet the Corneilles had served when their eldest daughter was married. Philippe clapped his hands and I felt a tingle of...something wash over me. Between one blink and the next the platters were filled with delicious scents and spicy sauces, with roasted meats and dainty pies, and a profusion of fruits I barely recognized filling an epergne in the center of the table. I had no hope of tasting every dish, but every time I protested that I was satisfied, Philippe urged me to one more bite until finally I laughed and said, "No more! No more!"

He frowned and waved the remaining food back to dead leaves. My stomach turned and I wondered if my dinner had changed back to the same within me. But I think it was only the shock.

"It's time to dance," he said. "My Lady Glace?"

His sister nodded without a word and the harpsichord began to play. Philippe rose and took my hand and led me out into the space before the fireplace.

"Why do you call her that?" I asked, when the movements of the dance seemed to call for conversation. "Why do you call her Lady Ice?"

"The answer is clear," he said, and then he laughed at his own joke.

I didn't think it was clear at all. Grace du Fortigny seemed anything but cold. Quiet, yes, and there was the matter of what the curse had done to her skin. But she seemed only to be waiting. Contained. Patient.

I would have enjoyed dancing with Philippe except that he, too, was waiting. He was neither quiet nor patient, just like my partners at the balls in town. They all were watching and hoping for some response I didn't know how to give. When our eyes met, Philippe's gaze seized on mine and I had to look away. I wanted to flee or faint, anything to escape. I focused on the rose, still tucked in the buttonhole of his coat. It was withered to a dark grayish purple now and, as I watched, a petal fell and drifted to the floor.

Philippe saw my eyes follow it and stopped, allowing the music to continue without us, until he gestured impatiently to his sister and it ceased.

He caught up my other hand as well to hold them close between us. "Alys, can you love me? Will you marry me?"

The question was no surprise this time. I steeled my courage and replied softly, "My lord, you do me great honor by asking, but I can give you no answer but the truth. I do not love you."

I felt his fingers stiffen where they held mine, but after a long pause he sighed and loosed his hold. "Someday I hope to change your mind. Goodnight."

Despite that word of farewell, Philippe followed me up the stairs this time and down the corridor to the door of my chamber. I hesitated, fearing that if I entered, he would follow me and then—what might happen then?

"Goodnight, Alys," came a voice from behind him. Lady Grace had followed us from the parlor. "It has been a tiring day, I think, and you must want to rest. Be assured that this chamber may serve as your refuge and we will not intrude."

I could see Philippe's muzzle twitch in that way I was coming to know was impatience, but he only lifted my hand to his lipless mouth in imitation of a kiss. "As my sister says, rest assured that you may be private here."

He turned away abruptly and disappeared into the dim shadows at the other end of the corridor. I smiled weakly at Lady Grace, ashamed to speak my thanks aloud and admit what my fears had been.

She stepped closer and held out her hand. I saw that it held a small bit of bread from dinner and took the offered gift.

"If you care to eat in the morning before Philippe rises, it's best to save something from dinner before it disappears." And then, with careful emphasis, "Philippe rarely rises before midday." And then she too turned and disappeared into the far reaches of the corridor.

There are many types of kindness in the world. I could only guess at what lay between Philippe and his sister, but Grace and I made a silent pact that night as allies.

The Guest

ONLY THE LEAVES TUMBLING along the garden path and the sharp tug at her garments told Grace of the bitter winter wind. Habit alone made her draw the edges of her cloak more closely together. The marble bench beneath her was as one with her featherbed. That was one gift of the curse. The deeper it took hold, the less she felt the chill.

She released the invisible ones from their task of cleaning the pathways. The wind-scattered leaves had long since erased the traces of her morning's walk. She could hear Philippe's morning growls drifting down from the upper story. The girl Alys was wandering aimlessly along the edges of the yard, trailing her fingers along the stone wall that marked the limits of Bettencourt's glamour. In the weeks since her arrival, Alys had fallen into the habit of long morning walks while Philippe was still abed.

She saw Alys pause at the small arched gateway and peer out past the bars. What did she see? Only the cloaking mist? Or would the glamour slip for a few moments and allow her sight of the forest? If, by some unlikely chance, a traveler passed by, would he be granted a brief glimpse of a young woman staring out from another world before his vision was once more clouded?

What did she think of Philippe's courtship? He was attentive to her every want. She no longer shrank from him when he led her into the dance, but neither did she invite more. Just as Grace had hoped, Philippe bent to the challenge of her cheerful diffidence. She had seen this game before.

Alys turned away from the gate and bent to examine the promise of a bud on the briar that grew beside it. Grace froze as a window slammed open from the story above and Philippe's voice rolled out across the yard, "Do not touch my rose!"

But the girl looked up and waved at him as she called back, "Of course not, Lord Philippe." She looked across at Grace and winked, as if she knew there was no danger when she hadn't transgressed.

"It's just his way," she'd said once when Grace had thought to reassure her. Alys's fascination with the rose would not be suspect. Philippe saw nothing strange in it for the rose was the bait that had brought her here.

How had they come to this? To a place where she must pin everything on the hope that a merchant's daughter could find something to love beneath her brother's rough ways? The beginnings were hard to trace, but it had been here, on this very bench, that they had all slipped over the cliff's edge and tumbled to disaster.

Had there ever been a time when matters might have gone differently? Would their parents have been able to temper his mercurial impulses if they had restrained him at the start? But they had bequeathed Bettencourt and all its glamours to Philippe. Fée were too long-lived to dwell in each other's pockets for a lifetime. She had been gathering the courage to leave and travel the many worlds herself. To escape Philippe's rages and jealousies if the opportunity came to do so safely. In those days before the curse, Bettencourt had drawn guests from far and wide. Balls and hunting parties and the coming and going of fée from the four corners of this world and others. Grace had waited and watched for her chance. The excuse of a visit, an invitation, anything Philippe would not dare to question before their guests. The fear that had bound her then was nothing to what trapped her now. Then, she had feared only for herself. Now she stood guard over something far more precious.

One glorious summer evening, Peronelle Latour had swept into their lives, trailing her retinue of chevaliers and changelings and attendants on her way to far Karasind. And in that retinue was her protégée Eglantine. Peronelle loved grand gestures and the echo of epic stories. Old blood called to old blood, she said. Eglantine and Philippe might ally two ancient names. She would return in a year to celebrate the wedding, should they suit. When Philippe saw Eglantine, nothing would do but that he must have her. And Eglantine seemed content to allow herself to be courted.

Eglantine had been a laughing, joyful guest. There was a hint of the same joy in Alys, though without the same confidence. And Philippe... Philippe had been enchanted. They all had been. For the first time Grace could remember, a stir of hope rose up that Philippe's heart might be caught. That this exquisite creature had coaxed his better nature to the fore. That Bettencourt might become a home and not a prison.

Grace loved her for the gifts she brought: for her generous spirit, for her laughing wit that sparkled like the gems that fell from her lips, for the light in her eyes that saw only the best in everyone. Grace loved her for the kindness that forgave Philippe's fumbling courtship, his jealous stumbles and his quick tempers. Grace loved how Eglantine saw into Philippe's little boy spirit and bent oh-so-slightly to keep him in check. Grace loved that Eglantine noticed how Philippe treated his quiet sister and loved how she used her talents when she could to deflect his anger away, sometimes catching it in her own hand. Grace loved— oh how she loved—and burned in secret with that love until she could lie to herself no more. She loved Eglantine for herself and not for the hope that she might tame Philippe.

When she recognized that truth, Grace felt her heart tremble in stillness, like a songbird trapped between two hands. Philippe must never guess what a fragile thing he held within his power. She had learned so early never to betray anything she cared for. Not to give him that temptation to crush something just for the hurt it would cause her. Grace told herself that if Philippe could win Eglantine's heart, then she could learn to keep this one thing hidden in hers for all their sakes.

 THE FRIEND

I CAME TO LOVE MORNINGS best, when there was no looming dread that Philippe might appear around any corner. When I could enjoy time under the sky without Philippe taking my arm and choosing the paths we would walk. He never threatened me or laid a hand on me in anger. Oh, he was impatient that I wanted so little of what he had to give. But he was just so very *present* and attentive, always offering me gifts and waiting eagerly for my delight. It was important that I be delighted. I had tired of the game of requesting exquisite dishes for our dinner, but if I asked for plain food or seemed indifferent Philippe would be moody all evening and send the food back to leaves and rubbish before we'd half-started, rather than leaving it for the invisible servants to remove.

Philippe could only transform what he could see. I learned that from Lady Grace. She never spoke a word against him, but I knew she feared him and the reason was no mystery. For me, he never showed worse than gruff impatience, but he needled his sister constantly. The only mystery was why she stayed. Did the curse bind them to this place? That would explain why they wanted company so badly.

Grace had shown me the trick of hiding a bit of bread from dinner in the folds of my skirt to save for the next day. She told me of his habits and interests. She tried to soften his edges to put me at ease but I was only truly at ease alone or with her. Not if Philippe were there. He seemed jealous of every word I spoke to Grace, every smile I gave her. And for her sake I learned to treat her as one of the invisible ones when he was present. We both bent to his moods, though Grace would never hear a word against him.

I stopped fearing that I would wake to find my chamber transformed into something new and strange while I slept, though I couldn't stop him from changing things when he hung in the doorway as he said goodnight.

I mentioned that I missed the gardens of home with their flowers and birdsong. So he created a vase of flowers for me every evening, and I must admire them and exclaim at their scent, though they had none and the petals felt like paper or wax. Nothing like the softness of the rose still kept hidden beneath my pillow. It was my other solace. I told it all my sorrows and fears: how I longed to see my sisters again and comfort my father. How I was oppressed by the weight of Philippe's unspoken desires. They were worse than the spoken ones.

Philippe made for me a caged bird to hang at my window—a brilliant poppinjay in appearance. But I saw that it hopped and chirped like a sparrow, and when I opened the cage it fluttered against the panes of the window until I found the latch and let it fly off into the mists past the wall, a bright flash of green and scarlet against the gray.

Indifference to his gifts brought only renewed efforts. He wanted to know that I was happy and grateful and comfortable. How could I be comfortable? He was so eager to supply anything I asked for. When I asked for a needle and thread so that I could remake some of the gowns more to my own taste, he produced a cabinet full of spools and laces and every size of needle one might want. But I found the thread was only a thin layer pasted on the spools, and the needles were sharp enough but had no eyes. And so I left my clothing as it was and said no more about sewing.

He tried so hard. Always, he would wait anxiously for my response, trying to catch my eyes, standing so closely that I couldn't breathe, always so unhappy if I failed to show delight. Why couldn't I? What woman wouldn't be delighted at a suitor who could truly give her anything she asked for? It seemed so little that he asked for in return.

I had lost track of the days. When had that happened? Only the nights seemed to change, with my dreams growing ever more vivid. My rose twined through my sleep, growing in strange shapes and throwing off a profusion of blooms, bright and changeable. The briars caught at my hands, not thorn-sharp, but clasping me in rough bark and drawing me down unknown pathways.

Yet the seasons sometimes made their way past the walls of Bettencourt. The wind in the yard sharpened from chill to freezing. It woke me from the haze of sameness. I walked the empty garden pathways and watched my breath steam in the air and filled my lungs until I coughed. A wild spirit took me and I lifted my skirts and began to run along the graveled path, all the way along the wall from the great gates past the briar and the smaller archway, around back past the empty stables. My hair had tumbled down from its pins and my chest was burning but I ran and ran, back to the empty fountain and the bench.

I tumbled to a stop beside Grace, sitting with her accustomed stillness. She was always there before me in the garden though I never saw her do anything but sit. When I could catch my breath, I said, "Today your cloak suits the weather!" She always wore the same white satin gown as when I'd first seen her. The skirts were heavy with pearls and glittered with small knots set with diamonds. Out of doors or in, it was covered by the same long cloak edged every-where with snow-white fox fur. I thought of the profusion of clothing that Philippe had created for me and wondered if she had others. "You never tire of that gown!"

"This is what it pleases Philippe for me to wear."

Ah, yes. It was easiest to choose to do what pleased Philippe. It was a gown designed for Lady Ice. But I couldn't help asking, "What would please *you*?"

For no more than a moment I saw a depth of longing in her eyes—her face itself was still as always. Then she turned to look up at Philippe's window. It was near time when he might be rising.

"Alys, have you everything you need? Can we do aught for your comfort that is lacking?"

It wasn't the first time she'd asked me that, as if she were daring me to be dissatisfied. *My freedom. To see my sisters again.* Unable to demand what I truly wanted, I'd always demurred. Today I couldn't find it in me to lie.

"Lady Grace…?"

Only a shift in the quality of her silence encouraged me to continue.

"Lady Grace, I could wish for an occupation." Having asked that much, I stumbled on. "I had the running of my father's house. I directed the servants, planned the meals, arranged for the comfort of his guests. I kept the keys of the storerooms and saw to the education of my sisters. I am not accustomed to being idle. It wears on me. Let me do something to help lighten your burdens."

"An occupation," Grace repeated.

She seemed to be amused, where Philippe would have been impatient and dismissive.

"What burdens do I have?" Grace continued. "The invisible ones do not need your direction. There are no keys to be kept. Philippe provides everything we need for the table. And there is no one here of an age for education. What occupation do you think could be found for you?"

She was lying about having no burdens. I could see them in every careful movement and silence. Henriette and Louise-Marie had rarely needed me for worse than bruised knees and bee stings, but here was a deep well of suffering. I ached to bring her ease, but I could recognize the sort of pain that could be borne only so long as it wasn't spoken. I looked helplessly around at the manor and grounds and began, "I've never had a hand for gardening…"

Did I imagine the brief flash of fear that crossed Grace's face?

"Philippe does not care to have the garden tended," she said.

"There are rooms we never use," I ventured. "They might be put to rights and made comfortable again."

"You need only tell Philippe which rooms you wish to use. Hasn't he said that you have only to tell him what you desire and it will be yours? What do you desire?"

"I want to know what I'm supposed to do. Why am I here?" There. I'd said it plainly: the question I'd never dared to ask Philippe.

I could see Grace picking her way among the possible answers. Would she slip sideways into the obvious? *You are here to pay your father's debt. You are here because your father picked a rose that didn't belong to him. You are here because we trapped you into giving us your company.* "Have we ever asked anything of you?"

"No." I shook my head in bewilderment. "Nothing, except for Lord Philippe's little joke about marrying him."

"Why do you think it a joke?"

It was an absurd question. "Because I'm nothing but a merchant's daughter. And you are..." *You are fée.* But I'd never said that aloud. I gestured at the imposing bulk of the manor of Bettencourt. "Someone like Lord Philippe doesn't marry someone like me. I know he's only teasing when he asks if I love him. And what's more, how can I love—"

"How can you love a beast?" Grace interrupted.

I frowned. I'd almost ceased to notice his appearance. I'd grown accustomed—to that and to his gruff manner and his moods. He was what he was. But I am what I am. "How can I love for the asking? How can I love him simply because he's there? I knew François Montardon all my life back home. He would have cherished me and given me a pleasant home. And yet when he asked if I loved him, I knew I had to refuse. What does Lord Philippe want? Is it only the words?"

"Do not concern yourself with what Philippe wants," she said. "But believe that he's in earnest when he asks, however clumsy his asking may be." And then she smiled stiffly. "As for an occupation, I have a thought."

She began to rise from the bench. Her slow movements suggested pain rather than pride and I stood to offer help, though I'd learned that she didn't care to be touched. I could understand that. This time she accepted my hand and a gentle pull to her feet. So cold she was!

"You shouldn't sit out here so long," I scolded as if she were Louise-Marie. "You'll catch your death!"

"Death will catch us all in the end, but the cold does me no harm," she replied and squeezed my fingers just a little before letting go.

THE JEALOUS LOVER

GRACE STARED AT THE hand before her. Her vision blurred for only a moment before pure will beat back the tears and she accepted the help to rise. A simple kindness could crack the armor she'd worn so long. That wouldn't do. She hadn't wept since the night Eglantine disappeared.

Fate kept turning back to that garden bench. How often had she sat there on the hard marble watching Philippe promenade through the gardens with Eglantine on his arm? He would nod to their guests as they passed, always being sure to be seen to best advantage. And Eglantine was part of that display. Grace had watched them and retreated into burning silence.

But Eglantine noticed the silences, the drawing back. At first, she came only to sit in quiet companionship. Her laughing heart couldn't imagine any peril. She had lived a different life, always sheltered against danger. Under her care, Grace had opened from a tight-closed bud to a blaze of unfurled petals, turning to Eglantine's sun. They had kissed: a meeting of lips against rose-petal skin, the intoxicating scent of her, the touch that promised so much more. They whispered secrets in the language of the flowers that dropped from Eglantine's tongue at every word. Grace could no longer be wise or cautious. Eglantine made her greedy and foolish and bold.

Philippe knew nothing—nothing certain. His loves always took a possessive turn. He only saw that Eglantine offered her smiles freely, and his words began to gnaw and rub.

"My sister Grace is always given to foolish infatuations. You mustn't let her exhaust your patience as she has mine."

"I love your childish fancies but it's time to look to your future. Things will change once you are mistress here."

"I've set the date. There's no need to wait for Peronelle's return. Leave everything in my hands. Who else can you trust?"

But Eglantine had put him off. "Nothing can be decided without Madame Latour. She's set in her ways and will want to see things done properly."

Grace could only watch as he wrapped his coils around Eglantine with honey-poisoned words. She knew her own counsels must sound desperate and strange. The invisible ones had no power to protect her against Philippe but they could whisper to her where he walked, warn her of his coming, give her brief moments for a private word.

The fatal moment had been here on this bench—nothing more guilty than taking each other's hands and gazing with wordless aching. "You must leave, soon," she had whispered to Eglantine "You've seen how he is, but you haven't seen his worst. You must leave before you're trapped here like me."

And Eglantine—gentle, brave, foolish Eglantine—in a miracle had believed her and said, "Not without you," the words coming in jasmine and bluebells.

But Philippe had seen.

Philippe had seen nothing more than hands clasped, but they could not have sworn they were innocent in their hearts. In Grace's memory, the garden was in riotous bloom. She remembered all the days with Eglantine as spring, though they had covered nearly the span of a year. Just as all the days since had seemed to be winter, though many years had passed. But that day—that one day—Grace was certain had been high summer, the boughs full of birdsong and a warm breeze bringing the vanilla scent of heliotrope.

The invisible ones had not betrayed her that day. How could they when they were part of herself? But she had released them from her attention. Her eyes were only for Eglantine. And so it was the crunch of Philippe's boots on the gravel walk that warned them, too late to snatch their hands back.

"What's this? What's this?" he said. The cheerful tone hid a steel edge. "My betrothed and my sister tête-à-tête?"

They weren't betrothed despite his confident claim. But Eglantine wisely didn't challenge him. "Your sister's hands were cold," she said. "Even on this summer day."

"My Lady Glace is always cold," Philippe said and took Eglantine's hand away from mine to lift it to his lips and raise her from the bench. "Come. If it's heat you want, you know where that's to be had."

Eglantine had given her one brief worried look as Philippe led her away.

Five days later, Philippe dismissed Eglantine's servants—the enchanted folk her godmother had left to attend her. He said he dismissed them. All she knew was that she woke one morning to find them gone.

"You have no need of them now that we're betrothed," he said over the breakfast table.

"We aren't—" she began, but he waved her protest away.

"Near enough, you must agree. I see no reason to have strangers eating us out of house and home, twiddling their thumbs in the stables and making trouble in the kitchen. Do you want for anything? Is there any way in which my people have failed to see to your comfort?" He seized the arm of a passing serving maid and she struggled not to spill the pitcher she carried. "Marie! Has your future mistress lacked in anything she requires?"

Bettencourt still had human servants in those days. Families who had always served the manor and put up with Philippe's moods for the sake of old loyalties.

"Your hospitality has been notable," Eglantine replied quickly. She spoke the words in emeralds and pearls to distract him. But not roses. She'd stopped speaking roses to him.

From that day on, Grace made certain that Eglantine was attended at all times by the invisible ones, so quietly that neither she nor Philippe knew.

It did not exhaust her then as it did now. The curse dragged at her magic. The further they slipped from flesh the greater the struggle. Grace had seen it even in Philippe's workings: a disused room entered unexpectedly with crooked floorboards and cracking plaster walls and broken branches where the furniture had been. And then the next day all was bright and new, the lapse forgotten.

When he enchanted rubbish into meat, did his bones ache the way hers did? Good, she thought. Let it pierce him with needles as it did her. Let it be a thorn in his flesh just like the ice in hers. And then she remembered that in Philippe's mood lay her only hope of salvation—hers and Eglantine's. And for a second time that day, she could have wept.

THE LIBRARIAN

How could it be so difficult to ask for employment? I'd been told I had only to ask and everything would be done for me, everything would be given to me. It felt ungrateful, but my days were filled with little but waiting for the sound of Philippe's shuffling, scraping tread in the hallways, the smell of musk that heralded his arrival, the awareness of his hovering presence, his constant solicitude. Was there anything I wanted? Anything I lacked? Anything he could shape from nothingness for me?

It made no difference to decline politely. He didn't hear or didn't heed. A bright carpet for my room. The carved mantelpiece changed to painted plaster. A gilded harp for me to play, taking up too much space in the parlor. I'd never learned to play the harp, only a few pieces on the harpsichord in the Corneilles' parlor.

For a while I tried to think of gifts to ask for. Useful things of comfort and familiarity. But always Philippe must improve them, refine them, elaborate them. The things I wanted were never sufficiently exquisite to serve as gifts. Always in the end Philippe gave me what he wanted to give, not what I wanted to have. Then he would turn to me and ask, "Are you pleased? Are you happy? Do you love me? Will you marry me?"

If it had always been the formal ritual it was at the first—the dinner, the dance, the question—I could have borne it. I could have continued to give him a gentle "no" in the same way I said "good night." But there was no moment of the waking day free of the shadow of that question. Days might pass and then, in an unguarded moment of surprised laughter or quiet pleasure it would come. "Alys, do you love me? Will you marry me?"

If it had only been the second question, I would have acceded only to make him happy. To stop his badgering. What did it matter? One must marry someone. But I wouldn't perjure my soul and say I loved him.

So I longed for distraction. I had meant it when I told Grace I wanted to share her burdens. Grace's quiet kindness was the only thing that made this life bearable. Instead, she gave me an occupation to lift *my* burden. And unlike Philippe's gifts, hers was welcome.

When we entered the manor, Grace led me down a corridor I'd never noticed before. I hadn't dared to explore the less used rooms. The house changed from day to day and the rooms we shared together seemed more *present* somehow. Not like the kitchens, disused and echoing when I examined them once through thick windows from the courtyard where they jutted off from the main buildings. Not like the portrait gallery I stumbled into when I took a wrong turning, where I spent a panicked hour trying to find the door back. It was months before I found that one again.

There were rooms I passed every day that failed to linger in my consciousness. Grace led me to one of those and opened an unnoticed door to reveal a library behind. It wasn't a large room—no larger than my bedchamber. The walls were thickly crowded with shelves. Bound volumes were heaped on tables higgledy-piggledy. I crossed the room to draw the curtains open and gasped at the wealth of books the light revealed. Bright covers in rich reds, blues, and greens with gilt lettering. Here was escape to fill my days, even if they were nothing more than dry philosophers and dusty histories.

"You asked for an occupation," Grace said. "I wish to have a catalog made of the contents of this room. A list of what stands on each shelf. The size, the color, the title and author, and what the contents might be. Philippe believes that a well-furnished library is an essential ornament for a noble house."

I opened the cover of the book that lay nearest to me on a table. At first it looked like ordinary text, but when I tried to read it, I realized the letters were random tracks, as if a mouse had stepped in ink, then run across the page. I looked up in surprise. "But...?"

"Philippe believes that a library filled with books is an essential ornament for a noble house," Grace repeated. "What fills the books is of lesser concern."

Thinking of the popinjay and the flowers at my bedside, I realized what Grace meant. Philippe had created the appearance of books with no concern for their substance. I reached for the next book and the next. At the fifth I found one with sensible words. *Les Contes Merveilleux.* I wondered if it held anything more marvelous than my own life.

"I wish," Grace repeated carefully, "to have a catalog made of the contents of this room. The nature of each book. Is that sufficient occupation to fill your time?"

"Yes," I said slowly, looking around. "I'll need a ledger book and ink."

"For that you must apply to Philippe."

PHILIPPE WAS MORE THAN eager to provide what I asked that evening after dinner. A pen of ivory with a silver nib. An ink well of cut crystal. And a ledger filled with what seemed the finest velum.

"What will you write, my treasure?" Philippe asked as I gathered up the tools.

"A...a catalog of your books." I felt shy of mentioning Grace's part. Philippe seemed to delight in thwarting anything that pleased his sister.

He looked bemused. Grace, as always, sat silently at the far end of the table.

My days took on a new routine. I woke from dreams in which a thorny briar grew limbs and writhed like a soul in pain, or like a creature rousing from sleep. My garden walks had become a less certain source of solitude. Philippe sometimes rose early now and would join me, guiding my steps. When we passed the rosebush at the gate, he would examine it for buds and pick them the moment they began to bloom, grumbling at how few they were.

"I think the rose would be happier with more sun," I suggested. From what the two had said, I knew the constant mist was part of the glamour that hid Bettencourt from the mortal world.

"Bah," Philippe replied. "I can have roses whenever I want, sun or no." And he stooped to pick up a dead leaf and turned it to a red rose before my eyes. But he tossed it aside onto the path. He never did that with the ones he picked, but wore them in a buttonhole until they had wilted and turned brown.

But now between noon and dinner, I had work to fill my hours. For the first few days, Philippe sat with me in the library, ready to jump up to bring the next volume and return each to its place. He would lean over my shoulder as I turned the pages to find some identifying mark to describe the enchanted books and harrumph noisily when I noted down, "No sense."

If he'd shown any interest in the books themselves, or even in the work of cataloging them, we might have become friends over the task. But his attention was all on me, a haunting, hovering presence that left me exhausted. When he lost interest, it was like silence after a storm. I spent no more than a few hours each day at the work. Longer than that and I would hear Philippe's tread in the corridor outside. The door would open and my attention would be claimed. Always politely. I never tested the limits of that politeness.

Most of the books were enchanted nonsense. Many of the rest were the sort I recognized from the shelves of Father's friends: printed books of law and collections of old tales, a manual of surgery set down in careful Latin, a slim volume of handwritten poems—or so I guessed from the setting of the lines, for the hand was cramped and difficult. Perhaps every ten days I would come upon something more interesting.

Once it was a book of household receipts with precise notes written in every margin. "Five receipts to dispel mice are less use than one good cat," one note read. And on another page, "A better way to ensure the rising of bread is to enchant one corner of the kitchen for warmth, but see that lazy kitchen maids do not sleep there." Elsewhere I found, "A young vine can be coaxed to grow in arabesques but an old vine will be stubborn." Coaxed? By magic or by a gardener? The book hinted of wonders.

Who had written those comments? The hand seemed the same in every case but it couldn't be Philippe's—not as he was. I saw how his clumsy paws strained to hold a fork and spoon at the table. Nor Grace, I thought. Not unless she had more skills than calling on her unseen servants. Had their parents been sorcerers as well? It was strange to think of Grace and Philippe having parents or any sort of ordinary life beyond our timeless present.

How did time pass for fée? Surely it hadn't always been like this. Was it the curse that left this place unchanging from day to day? Why had they been cursed? The fée that I'd met in the wood outside the gates had said so little. Was it only the transformation of their flesh? If Philippe was doomed to long unchanging days trapped in this manor with only a sister he disdained, no wonder that he had arranged for company—even the company of an unwilling captive such as me. *Do you love me? Will you marry me?* Perhaps it was no more than a plea not to abandon him to the endless years. And what of Grace? Why did she stay? I could feel her deep unhappiness. Was it no more than loyalty to Philippe? I could understand such loyalty if the two were close. And that made me think of Father and Henriette and

Louise-Marie. How long had it been since I'd brought them to mind?

I cried myself to sleep that night and told the rose I wanted to go home. In my dreams, the rose grew a face that watched me with sorrowful eyes but never said a word.

How MANY DAYS HAD I been cataloguing? I counted time only by the number of true books I found. I wanted to keep the ledger of household receipts in my chamber to read in odd moments, but when I applied to Grace for permission—permission seemed advisable—I was told, "Leave all as you found it."

"Shouldn't I sort out the true books from the false?" I'd asked.

"No, leave all as you found it."

But one day I found a book that tempted me to disobedience. It was small—no more than the size of my hand—and bound in bright green leather the color of a new-furled leaf. Small enough that perhaps I had simply overlooked it before. There it stood, on the shelf I had been cataloging the day before. An armorial cinque-foil was tooled into the cover between scrolling vines. On the title page, in flowing manuscript, the words: *The Language of Roses.* Each page held a flower: sometimes a single bloom, sometimes a cluster, sometimes simple, sometimes with a profusion of petals. Each was hand-tinted in a wild riot of colors—all the colors one might expect in a rose garden and more besides. Below each painting was a brief inscription. "The sign of truest love" under a flower so dark and red it might have been heart's blood. "A token of returned affection is requested" with the image of a cluster of bright yellow flowers with golden centers. Between two pages I found a pressed flower, so faded its colors couldn't be discerned, but the painting it marked was of a pure white flower brushed at the heart with hyacinth blue and the inscription read, "I would share a path with you throughout the wide world."

One bloom to each page, each different, and then midway through the volume they turned to nothing but printed outlines of uncolored flowers with space below to write. Not a manual then, but a journal? I knew about the flower game that was played in the courts and salons of Paris. We knew it in a simpler form at home, where flowers rarely told of any sentiment not already known. But this was different.

I thought of the undying rose that lay beneath my pillow and how the colors seemed to shift. Seemed? No, I knew for certain that they changed, although my mind had always slid sideways from that fact before. My father had said he picked a red, red rose, but the one I selected from his gifts laid out on the table had been pink. At the time, I thought it poetic exaggeration. Father had always been free with truth for the sake of a good story. But the morning I set out from home, I was certain it had been red at the heart. I'd seen the rose in my dreams so often that I'd convinced myself the shifting colors were half-remembered visions. And there was enchantment enough in the flower's stoic persistence that a change of color had seemed of little moment.

Red, Father had said. Had it been dark heart's-blood? Or bright cherry? Or the color of brick? I thumbed through the pages of the book, trying to think what it might have been saying. My eyes lit on the design I remembered from the morning I left home: a warm shell-pink brushed with red at the center. "Have courage, all will be well." A message? But from whom? From Philippe?

I hadn't meant to defy Lady Grace and take the book away with me, but somehow it was still in my hand when I closed the library door behind me. I heard Philippe's shuffling step from several rooms away. With a pang of guilt, I tucked the book into a fold of my skirts and tiptoed off in the other direction to find the stairs up to my chamber. I slipped the book under my pillow beside the rose before hurrying back to find Philippe and distract him with a request for dinner.

CHAPTER FOURTEEN

THE THIEF

EVEN IF GRACE HAD been in the habit of talking to others, she would have found it hard to say aloud that Alys's presence had become a joy and a comfort in Bettencourt. A comfort even beyond the hope she brought that the curse might end. But there was no one to speak to besides Philippe and Alys herself, and so she kept silent but could admit it freely in her thoughts where there was no fear that Philippe would turn that joy against her. The joy was not unmixed. The long years when Philippe had been her only company had passed quickly. Every day with Alys brought some small memory to mark the time: a question, a kindness, an unexpected smile, the possibility that she had caught Philippe's heart as no other had succeeded in doing. Not even Eglantine. A hope that his attentiveness and care would be returned.

And there *was* hope. Who would not love Alys? She wasn't Eglantine—she was shy and hesitant where Eglantine had been bold and merry. Where Eglantine had treated Philippe's moods as of no moment, Alys had patience and an instinct for turning them aside. Philippe had loved Eglantine as he loved all bright beautiful things he longed to possess. But his care for Alys was more tender, more patient. Did Alys see that? Did she love him in return? Grace didn't dare think what a trap it could be to love one such as him. Not when Eglantine's life hung in the balance. It needn't be a love for the ages, so long as it would suffice for Peronelle. It need only be a love that would fit the shape her curse had left for a key.

Every morning Grace's limbs were stiffer and heavier. Every evening it took more focus to hold the invisible ones to their tasks as they served the meal and cleaned the table, prepared the rooms, and then played sweet music when Philippe invited Alys to dance. Every night the hopeful question and then the quiet, reluctant refusal. Then Grace would summon them for one last task to light the others up to bed. When they had gone, she would sit for hours sometimes, gathering the strength to rise. There had been nights she'd slept at the table, cheek pillowed on her arms.

That would never do. Philippe must never know. If there was one law that ruled her life it was that Philippe must not know. He mustn't know how many of his gifts lay ignored in Alys's chamber. He had so little sense for what a woman like her would want. Philippe must not know that Alys kept the stolen rose and whispered her secrets to it in the dawn. His sorcery could not reach farther than his senses, and he'd given his word to Alys that he wouldn't intrude. But how much could either of them trust his word?

Philippe must not know. How had they kept their secrets so long, she and Eglantine? Grace had kept them with silence, as always. But Eglantine had masked them with bountiful unstinting joy. She offered her smiles and words to all the world, as freely as she dropped jewels and flowers. Philippe had jealousies but not suspicions. He begrudged every smile Eglantine gave to anyone but him, but as a miser hoards gold, not as one watching for thieves.

Thief, she had been, stealing kisses from her brother's intended, with the invisible ones set on watch. Philippe must not know. No one must know who could betray them. She grew careless, for Eglantine's touch took her out of her senses and into a dream. A dream they began to plan in truth. They must leave. They must flee beyond the reach of Philippe's sorcery. Could they wait until Peronelle's return? Madame Latour had powers that could stand against his if she were prepared, but the days closed in around them. Philippe was growing more insistent. He wanted the betrothal, the promise, the contract. He wanted Eglantine's word that she was his.

And so they had planned escape. It was a simple plan—too simple, perhaps. Grace would leave to visit…it hardly mattered. An old friend. A neighbor. She would ride out accompanied by only a groom. She could give one of the invisible ones a solid enough form to wear livery. She would announce her plan to return the next day.

But instead, she would wait with the horses outside the garden gate after dusk. When all the household had retired, Eglantine would join her there. They would ride all night and cross between the worlds. By dawn they would be free. Free to go where? It didn't matter. But Philippe must not know. Not until they were safely away.

Grace waited in the shadows of the wood. And waited. And waited until she heard the soft crunch of dainty feet on gravel paths. Silence and the faint, slow creak of an iron gate. Why hadn't she thought to have the invisible ones grease the hinges? More footsteps on the gravel, heavier this time. A voice so angry and controlled it seemed a growl.

"Where are you going, my love?"

Had someone betrayed them? Or had it simply been the misfortune of a glance from an upper window that saw a cloaked figure crossing the garden?

"Where are you going all alone at night?"

What answer could Eglantine have given that would have satisfied him? Grace would have faced him silently, letting his suspicions wash about her until he'd spent his wrath. Another might have spun a tale of moonlit walks and restless dreams then let him lead her back inside. But Eglantine had no guile. She spoke her truth to the world as freely as the flowers and gems that fell from her lips.

"I'm leaving, Philippe."

"Leaving? But you are mine." He said it almost in confusion, as a child might. "This is your home now."

"No, Philippe."

He had spoken as a child and she addressed him as one, but that was no way to manage him. Grace clenched her hands into fists and pressed them against her mouth in helpless silence, imagining them face to face on the other side of the wall.

"No, Philippe, I'm leaving. We aren't suited to each other. We never were."

"You will *stay!*" Anger had replaced bewilderment. "You will stay."

Grace felt a wave of sorcery pass through the world, more powerful than any she had known before. Then silence. And then one set of heavy footsteps receding along the gravel path back toward the manor.

She sank to the ground with her back against an ancient oak and wrapped her arms around her knees to keep herself in one piece, and waited. And waited. And waited for the dawn.

CHAPTER FIFTEEN

THE CONFIDANTE

SHE CAME TO ME in my dreams—the flower-faced woman—reaching out to me with gnarled bark-clad fingers, not in menace but pleading. Her mouth worked constantly but no sound came. Her petals deepened from pink to a deep violet streaked with gold. On waking, I thought of the small green book I'd hidden beneath my pillow. My rose lay beside me, wearing the colors I'd dreamed. The change itself no longer surprised me. And now I had a key to its meaning. I leafed through the paintings. There—not a perfect match. In the picture, the center was more gold and speckled. Below the image was written, "I desire conversation."

I surprised myself by laughing. When had I last laughed so freely?

"Conversation, is it?" I said aloud. I held the flower up and slid off the bed to curtsey to it.

"Perhaps we should be introduced. I am Alys Levesque. I'm pleased to meet you, Lady Rose."

Before my eyes, the colors shifted slightly, or so I thought.

I'd spoken my heart to Lady Rose so often in the lonely night but never before with the thought of return. I found myself telling the flower my whole story: Father's visit to Bettencourt, how he'd picked the flower, and how I had returned here in his place.

"I don't blame *you*, my dear Lady Rose," I said. "You were plucked away as unwillingly as I was."

But that wasn't true. I had been willing, as far as a choice was given to me. When Father picked the rose, she'd had no choice at all. Then I felt foolish for speaking to a flower and tucked it back beneath the pillow where the invisible servants would leave it in peace.

THOSE SERVANTS HAD LAID out a new dark green walking suit—almost a riding habit, with braid and buttons, except not so long in the skirts. Usually, I went walking in my favorite brown woolen dress, but today I'd dallied too long to take my morning walk before Philippe rose, so I chose a lighter gown: a striped silk in sap-green and daffodil-yellow, trimmed with ruching of the same material cut cross-wise to the pattern. It gave the appearance of a thorny vine winding up the front of the skirt and along the robings. The dress had seemed too fine when Philippe first presented it to me and I knew he'd been disappointed that I hadn't worn it the day it first appeared. But now it seemed perfect for a day that had begun in conversation with a flower. I could make up for that disappointment.

Of all the strange things in this place, it had been easiest to grow accustomed to the touch of the unseen servants as they tugged at corset laces and fastenings, then combed and pinned my hair in place. If they had been Philippe's creatures, I might have cringed even at their impersonal touch, wondering how closely they were directed. But even if it had been Grace herself, instead of her spirits, I would have welcomed the care. We had grown easy together in that way of long companionship.

When I came into the parlor, both Philippe and Grace turned to face me from opposite ends of the table. I froze. We rarely took breakfast together, but it seemed they were waiting for me. Grace sat still with her hands in her lap. Philippe was toying with his fork impatiently. A frown faded from his face.

"You tarried long this morning," he said evenly.

My thoughts flitted back to my conversation with the rose. "Yes. I...I had dressed entirely then changed my mind and had it all to do again." That wasn't enough explanation for the entire delay, but it was all I could think of. I smoothed my hands down the ruffled edges of the skirt. "Forgive me for keeping you waiting." I hoped it was the right apology to give.

The fork slipped from Philippe's clawed fingers, or perhaps he let it fall. "I had a surprise planned," he said. "But you've worn the wrong dress. It's no use now."

The walking dress? I hadn't thought there was any special meaning to it. "I could change again," I offered.

"No, no, you've made your choice. Perhaps the chance will come again, perhaps not."

Whatever chance he meant was not forthcoming. If I asked, he'd answer in teasing hints, and the longer I kept up the game, the more frustrated he'd be when I finally let it go.

"Shall we eat?" Grace said.

At Philippe's grunted assent, the servants produced tea and pastries. I still had never caught them at their work. Always, the dishes would arrive between one blink and the next. I broke and buttered a roll and was in the middle of pouring tea for Philippe when he asked, "Who were you talking to this morning?"

The tea splashed over the lip of his cup and I paused a moment too long. "No one."

"I heard you, laughing and chattering away in your chamber."

He made it sound teasing but my heart quickened. Were the unseen servants his spies after all? Or had he been listening in the corridor all that time? How much had he heard? What would he believe?

"Perhaps," Grace said, "she was teaching the popinjay to talk."

I gave her a look of gratitude. The popinjay had never done more than twitter like the sparrow it had begun, and it was long since flown, but Philippe had never asked about it after the initial gift. The answer seemed to satisfy him.

To mollify Philippe, I spent the morning in his company, allowing him to show me a dusty collection of curious stones and seashells until time for the midday meal. After that, not even habit gave me an excuse for solitude in the library, but we must finish the tour of his collection.

Philippe's enthusiasms were exhausting: the hours spent attending to his every word. He would quiz me at odd moments. If I lost the thread, he would sigh and tell me how sorry he was for being tedious. It was the opposite of tedium. If he had taken any joy in the things he showed me, I would have shared that joy. But instead, I must coax him from his sulks and allow him to twine his furred arm in mine and lead me about the room, pulling out drawers and opening cabinets. When at last he tired and I could slip up to my chamber to dress for supper, it was with a mixture of relief and guilt. Philippe seemed so very lonely, but it was a depth of loneliness I didn't know how to fill.

The Briar

His hold is slipping. I feel it in my roots and in my sap. I feel it in the swelling of my buds and the prickling of my thorns. I feel flesh returning beneath the bark. I never feared him enough—that cloud that came between me and my sun. I never feared anything. I never feared Madame, even knowing the power she wielded. She enfolded me in that power like a tight-wrapped blanket and I could never fear. But neither could I grow. I was too eager to reach my limbs up to the sky and open every leaf. First, I should have learned fear.

In the dark, I've learned to fear.

Fear, when I felt Madame come and go again, never seeing me there. Never recognizing me. Isn't that the way of it? That we fail to recognize what our children become? She wanted her daughter back and I was no longer the daughter she knew. All her thoughts were of revenge against those who took a child who no longer existed.

Fear at what *he* might do while I stood helpless and rooted. Fear every time I feel his touch, plucking and breaking and warning me of what he might do if he chose.

Fear that my sun would blink out and leave me eternally in the cold and dark. I fear that now. Even as his grasp weakens, so does her light.

Two things are pushing out the fear. Hope comes in the voice that speaks to me, the gentle hands, the listening heart. Hope that she will hear and understand. That she will find the key to our prison. But something deeper and more strongly rooted grows entwined around fear and hope.

I feel his rough grasping hands, but his hold is slipping. And in the dark, I've learned to hate.

THE INVISIBLE ONES

IT WASN'T TRUE THAT every day was exactly like every other. I could hardly count what appeared on the dinner table as a change, though. One day there would be a roast of lamb, the next a delicate ragout. At first, I tried to request fish on fast days, but I lost track of the calendar. Philippe was always delighted to provide whatever dish I asked—the more elegant the better. It was a small matter in which to make him happy, even when it was a burden.

Other things changed. The manor grounds seemed locked in unending autumn, but that was only the barren flower beds and the way leaves wilted and dried if they came over the wall. Beyond the walls and through the great iron gates I could catch glimpses of a change in the seasons when the mist parted. Now the silhouette of bare branches against an ashen sky; now a flash of spring green, now a flurry of crimson leaves proclaiming fall. Those glimpses came more often now. That, too, was a change. Or perhaps the changing trees outside the gates were Philippe's doing.

I tried to set the clues in order. How long had I been here? One year? Two? More? Or only months? Were my sisters married by now? Had they started families of their own? Did they ever wonder what had become of me?

Two things made steady progress that I could see: my catalog of the library, shelf by shelf, and the way that the beast overshadowed the man in Philippe's person. It would have made sense if I'd thought him more monstrous at first and then seen that lessen with familiarity. I became accustomed to the shape of the snout that murmured his eternal question, the sharp horny claws that scratched me in passing no matter how careful he was. But I watched him change. The eyes that watched me closely every evening over dinner. The paw that took my hand when he led me out into the dance. How his limbs moved in ever more beast-like angles. It didn't matter. He was always simply Philippe. My "no" had never been because he was Philippe, but because I was Alys.

Grace didn't change—not in face or form. Only in the increasing care and slowness of her movements. And my Lady Rose never changed—except in the colors that welled and shifted, sending me hunting through the little green book to read her meaning. That is, the rose kept tucked beneath my pillow never changed, but I knew it was the same Lady Rose who haunted my dreams and grew ever more substantial and more frantic. Who begged for me to… do what? I didn't know. I only knew that her secret company made my nights bearable, just as Grace did my days.

But when I thought on it, there was another change. Just as the wall of mist parted more often now, the magic that wove through the manor wavered and flickered more often. Bettencourt had far more stairways and rooms than the ones we inhabited. There had been days when I explored the unused spaces and found them filled with glittering treasures and fine furnishings. Now many rooms stood emptied of their riches. I thought of how Philippe could only transform one thing for another and wondered what substance he used for his gifts and our meals.

One morning I turned a corner by idle chance and found the portrait gallery I'd once stumbled upon. Now it was bare floors, peeling paper, the picture frames so thick with dust that I could see nothing of the faces beneath.

I asked about it that evening as we dined. "Why are so many of the rooms neglected? Where have the furnishings gone?"

"Neglected?" Philippe said in a rumbling voice. "Whose fault is that?" His eyes narrowed and he snarled at Grace where she sat unmoving. "Where are your servants that should be about their business? You disappoint our guest."

I tensed and dinner felt like a stone in my belly. I should have thought. I hadn't meant to raise his anger, for of course it would fall on Grace.

Philippe slammed one curled paw on the table. "We cannot have *neglect* in this house, my Lady Ice. Or perhaps you enjoy living in filth?"

With a gesture, the remaining food on Grace's plate changed to a smear of stinking manure.

Grace set her fork and knife aside and said, "Any room that you desire shall be cleaned. You have only to ask."

"I shouldn't need to ask," Philippe said and pushed away from the table, rising awkwardly to offer me his arm. His voice softened. "Shall we dance?" But he threw one more glare at his sister. "I shouldn't have to *ask*."

I thought I saw Grace wince, but it must have been only my sympathy. The music started up from invisible hands and Philippe led me through the figures, ending as always with that pleading question, "Alys, do you love me? Alys, will you marry me?"

In that moment, I was so tired. I wanted relief from his endless pestering. I wanted to protect Grace from his rages. I wanted to put an end to this eternal game. Would it make such a difference to answer yes? I saw Grace watching us. I felt her quivering in anticipation, though as always she was perfectly still. What did *she* want me to say? But long repetition brought the words to my tongue. "No, Philippe."

When I was alone in my chamber and had changed my gown for a nightdress, I sat at the dressing table and began weeping silently. My brushes and things were still scattered about. The servants hadn't arranged them carefully in a row as usual. I picked one up, but before I could raise it, unseen hands took it and began stroking slowly through my hair. I closed my eyes so that the absence of a figure in the glass behind me wouldn't cause my stomach to turn. If you'd asked me, I'd have said I hated being fussed over, but it wasn't true. It was only Philippe's sort of fussing I hated.

I missed how my sisters and I would dress each other in the morning, leaving the maids to other work. I missed them so fiercely now, with the brush slipping softly from crown to shoulders and beyond. It was familiar and comforting in the same way. It made no demands, expected no response. When I'd first come to Bettencourt, I would have called the attentions of the invisible ones impersonal, but now I could imagine Grace standing behind me, offering me courage and sympathy. And then, when my sobs had quieted and my tears had dried, the brushing stopped.

Only then did I think how unexpected that gesture had been, to be offered unasked. That was another slow change. When I first arrived, the invisible servants had been a constant presence: setting everything to rights, attending on me, cleaning the rooms. And then it changed and, I thought, perhaps it had been courtesy alone when they stopped doing things unasked and waited for my commands. It was hard to become accustomed to speaking to empty air the same as I would to the servants in Father's house.

But now I noticed things left undone. It wasn't only the dusty gallery and the echoing rooms. Even in the rooms we occupied, clear direction was needed to keep things in order. Now I wondered: how much of Grace's stillness was a hoarding of her sorcery? Had Philippe grown more clumsy and impatient or did I simply notice it more? How much of the manor was real, apart from the sorceries placed on it? Was it like the library, with no more than one book in ten a true one? Why were those magics failing now? Would the passage of time mean a slow slide into dereliction and decay?

After I'd washed the traces of salt tears from my cheeks, I took out the rose as I did every night before sleep. Her spicy scent filled my dreams but Lady Rose was nowhere to be seen. I only heard a faint voice calling to me from within a spiny thicket. I couldn't understand the words, only that there was something I must answer, something I must do. In sleep, I walked through empty gardens filled with pale flickering ghosts of flowers. Then Lady Rose stood beside me, taking my hand with her bark-covered fingers, leading me somewhere, but there was no path.

CHAPTER EIGHTEEN

THE WATCHER

WHY DID YOU RETURN, Peronelle? Was it only to witness the triumph of your revenge? It was always meant as revenge, wasn't it? Never justice. Never hope. The calendar was engraved on your heart, there was no need to see it accomplished. Three days and three and thirty years. You knew to the moment when it would be complete. Why did you return? Did you fear that somehow they would escape your doom? Oh, but Peronelle, wasn't that what you said you wanted? That they would be redeemed? That they would know the same pain you knew, and in that suffering they would be free? You never could recognize pain unless it looked like your own, just as you never recognized happiness in a different guise. You thought Philippe would be my prince and so you never understood that he could be both prince and beast at the same time. You were never afraid of anyone, so you couldn't see Grace's fear beneath her silence. You punished them, not for their true selves, but for the walls they raised to protect those selves. Yes, even Philippe did not deserve what you called down on him. Who made you their judge, you who have sown as much pain as any of them? Who will judge you, Peronelle?

You can feel the power of the du Fortignys weakening, can't you, Peronelle? This isn't the deliberate lifting of the glamour over Bettencourt. This isn't the opening of the gates to entice visitors. This is the curse tearing their power into ragged shreds. Do you know what will happen when the span of time is complete, Peronelle? When Philippe loses his last trace of humanity and Grace moves no more? Can you guess the fate of Bettencourt and all that lies within its walls? Do you care?

Why have you left your tower and its gardens to wait there in the woods, Peronelle? You built Tourdespine again and filled it with treasures from the ends of the earth. Once more you gathered a retinue of chevaliers and changelings and your choice of guests from among the fée. Why do you wait alone beneath the dark boughs of the trees tonight, watching Philippe's glamours thin and fade like mist in a summer sun?

What have you seen when those defenses slip? A barren courtyard with empty gardens? A once-proud mansion now rotten at its heart—not only in its soul but in its very fabric? Or do Philippe's illusions still hold that much? Can you see through to the truth, Peronelle? Ah, but when have you ever cared for truth? Nothing is ever as it seems.

You were so certain you knew the truth, weren't you, Peronelle? When you returned from far Karasind and found your darling gone, you knew who to blame. And there was Philippe du Fortigny, sneering at your despair and saying foul things that could not be allowed to stand. He was worse than a beast, wasn't he, Peronelle? And there stood Grace du Fortigny at his side, seeming all cold and unconcerned. What could she know of a mother's heartbreak? Oh, you claimed a mother's grief then, didn't you? Had you ever before thought of the grief of mothers and daughters? But Grace would offer no scrap of hope, no hint of where your beloved child had gone. You called her as silent and uncaring as stone and she said nothing in her own defense. You couldn't know what had become of Eglantine, but you knew who stood in your way. And you would make them pay.

They have paid, Peronelle—paid and paid across the years. Soon they will pay the final price for your sorrow and rage. But you will not be content until you see it done. How much longer will it be?

There, through the mist, do you see the girl, Peronelle? Have you thought what will become of her when the end comes? Do you care? Have you become as cold and cruel as your curse? Or is your only concern that she might break the spell? That, after all these years, she could be the key that allows them to escape? Is that why you return again and again to wait and watch?

Call to her, Peronelle. When the glamour thins and fades, call to her and ask if she can love a beast. See if she will thwart your vengeance at the last.

CHAPTER NINETEEN

THE VISITOR

I WOKE IN DARKNESS WITH a thorn stabbing my palm where I grasped Lady Rose's stem. Why had I reached for it in my sleep? Moonlight blazed across the floor of the chamber. That was enough to bring me full awake. I crossed to the window and looked out. The gray clouds had parted overhead, leaving an expanse of pearl-studded velvet black. In all the time I'd been at Bettencourt, I'd never seen more than passing glimpses of the moon through the enchanted glamour that cloaked the manor.

"Did you wake me to show me this?" I whispered to the rose.

I could see shades of dark and light scudding across the petals, just like the wisps of cloud drifting across the moon's surface, but the dim light muted the colors too much to read.

"Please light a lamp," I asked the unseen servants. For the first time I could remember there

was no response at all. I took a spill of kindling
from the hearth and blew a coal into flame, then
turned up the lamp wick and lit it. In the soft
glow of the flame, the rose settled into a brilliant white with streaks of purple at the heart.
As I watched, the purple spread throughout the
petals, all the way to the edges, and a golden
glow grew from around the stamens. I remembered that one: *I desire conversation*. But what had
the first colors said? I reached under the pillow
and drew out the little green book.

A visitor, it said. A visitor who wanted to talk
to me? But there were never any visitors here at
Bettencourt. Should I go wake Philippe and tell
him? He didn't care for surprises.

Even as I thought it, the rose flashed back to
the purest white. A caution? A white rose had
so many meanings: innocence, purity…silence. It
was listed last on the page, but it was the only
one that made sense.

"This must be a secret?" I asked. Our conver-
sations had become puzzles to solve, the colors
shifting more quickly in response to my questions. Now Lady Rose showed the pattern for
conversation again, then once more *a visitor*.

"A visitor will come," I repeated slowly, "that
I must speak to, but keep the conversation a
secret?" A thorn pricked my thumb. "Keep the

visitor a secret?" No remonstrance this time. "But how can anything be kept a secret in this place from Grace and Philippe?"

The colors of the flower became confused and muddied. I could almost feel Lady Rose's frustration. Slowly, pulsingly, as if with great effort, the petals crimsoned and then turned almost black. I looked through the pages for the key. A black rose...*death*? For me? Or for someone else? But at the bottom of the death page was a scribbled note. *Sometimes this refers instead to the clock.*

I looked to the clock on the mantel but it had never told the time. It was one of Philippe's ensorcelled decorations like all the nonsense books in the library. The clock...

I remembered a neighbor once planting what she called a garden clock with flowers that bloomed at different times of day. None of them had been roses. I searched again through the book. There was an outline of a clock face sketched onto one page but no painted blossoms. No text at all, as if it had never been finished. Yet if a black rose signaled the time, what time could it mean but night? I was to go meet a visitor at night for a secret conversation. Now? I thought how the moonlight had pierced the magical mist. Was Philippe's power thin tonight? Was that why Lady Rose could speak more freely? Might it mean an opening to the outside world, like the day I arrived?

Of a sudden, the matter seemed urgent. I put on my slippers and tied a robe over my nightdress and eased out into the corridor, then down the stairs and through the hallways toward the front doors as quietly as might be. As I passed the parlor my heart nearly stopped. Grace sat slumped over the dining table, as still as death. I rushed to her side, but when I would have touched her shoulder, I saw her breath stir a strand of hair that had fallen across her face. Only exhausted, then. I wouldn't disturb her rest only to reassure myself. That little I could do for her, though I wished I could do more. I tiptoed out and slipped through the door to the court-yard as silently as I could.

Moonlight silvered the gravel paths. Now that I stood there in the cold and dark the sense of urgency drained away. What was I meant to do? Lady Rose had sent me here; did she have another message for me? I felt exposed to view as I crossed the empty gardens to where the briar stood beside the small arched door. I glanced up at the windows of Philippe's chamber but there was no light, no stirring of the curtains.

The briar had grown since the last time I saw it. The trunk was thicker and the branches swelled in knotted curves. Buds tipped the stems—more than I'd ever seen at one time before—but none unfurled to speak to me. The pale light showed the grounds empty, as they always were. Wherever my meeting was to be, it must be outside the walls.

I followed the path to the wide expanse of the main gates and peered out though the iron bars. Would I need to open them to complete my errand? I remembered how the hinges had screamed the day I arrived. But no. There at the far side of the clearing stood a cloaked figure, touched by just enough moonlight to pick her out of the shadows. Though her face was hidden, I recognized the same lady I had seen at my arrival, how long ago? As I stepped up to the gate, she came forward, pushing back her hood and looking at me curiously as if I were the unexpected vision instead of her.

"Why are you here?" she asked.

Here at the manor, or here tonight at the gate? I wondered. It would be absurd to say, *Lady Rose sent me,* so I covered my confusion by returning the question. "Why are *you* here?"

"The time approaches. I would see the curse finished."

Was this what Lady Rose had sent me for? "Why are they cursed? What did they do to deserve such a fate?"

The woman's eyes bored into me as our gaze met through the bars. "How has the beast been treating you?" she asked. "Is he kind? Is he tender?" Her voice hung balanced between scorn and curiosity.

"He is…" I wondered what to say.

"Does he love you?" the woman interrupted. Her voice sounded eager, hungry.

"He…" Again I hesitated. For all the repetitions of Philippe's proposal, it had always concerned my feelings, never his own. "He has asked me to marry him."

"Ah," she said. "And what did you answer?"

"He asks me every night if I love him and if I'll marry him. Every night I tell him no, I don't love him."

Now the woman's voice twisted bitterly. "Of course not. Who could love such a beast?"

"It isn't that," I protested. How could she understand what I'd only found words for recently? *Not because he's Philippe, but because I'm Alys.*

"Philippe can be kind and charming." *When he chooses.* "He's attentive and gives me everything I ask." I pushed out of memory all the other things. The sudden spite he would turn on his sister. How he would turn gold into dross when his patience faltered. Oh, he would give me anything I asked, but I'd learned what to ask for. "He loves me as he is able."

"Time has run out," the lady said. "He's had his chance. Three days, three years and thirty he's had to win a heart such as yours. That should have been enough. Now the curse will run its course." Her voice was harsh and unforgiving.

My body felt suddenly hollow, as if the ground had fallen away and left me behind. So this was why I'd been brought to Bettencourt. Why Philippe pestered me with questions every night. Why Grace had guided me with hints. What Lady Rose had tried to tell me. I was to be the key to break their curse. They *needed* me. I thought of Father, lured into the manor, all to set my fate in motion.

"How dare you!" I said, before I thought about the peril of saying such words to a sorceress. "How could you set such a task for me!" I stepped back as she advanced. She'd said that her magic couldn't reach within the walls of Bettencourt, but Bettencourt's magic was failing.

"Do you know what they did to Eglantine, my beloved child?" she said. "A year and a day she was to be their guest—a year and a day for love to grow between her and Philippe du Fortigny." She spat the name out as if it were made of gall. "When I returned, she'd vanished and they would tell me nothing of her fate. He raged and sneered and called her filthy names and said she'd betrayed him. And *she*—"

I could tell it was Grace that she meant.

"She stood there silent through it all, with no word of compassion or regret. A stone would have been more soft. And these were who I thought to join with in alliance!"

More of her words came back from that first time we met before these gates. "So you turned him to a beast and her to stone? I thought you said your magic was to—" I cast my mind back. "To reveal things as what they truly are."

"They cursed themselves. I only set it in their flesh. Three days beyond three and thirty years they had to prove that they could love and inspire love. Love freely given and freely returned and the spell would break. Most could have managed such a little thing, but not those two."

"But that's not true!" I protested. "That's not how they are at all! I know—"

"Ask them what happened to Eglantine." Her voice cut across my objections. "You will know them by their answer."

Eglantine. Should the name have been familiar? A cloud scudded across the moon and I looked up to see the mist close in. When I turned my gaze back to the gate, I could see nothing past the iron bars. I turned and hurried back to the manor, shivering now with cold and afraid my absence might be noticed, by the unseen servants, if no one else.

I paused as I passed the parlor doorway but Grace was no longer there. Was it true what the strange fée had said? That I'd been brought here to fall in love with Philippe and break the spell? I might believe it of him, but not that Grace could be so calculating. Was it possible that all her friendship and quiet kindness had been false?

Ask them what happened to Eglantine. I would ask her. I must know.

CHAPTER TWENTY

THE ACCUSER

GRACE WOKE TO THE familiar sense of gratefulness and regret for another day in her treacherous body. A few hours' rest had let her climb the stairs at last but now she had no strength to descend for her brief, private time with Eglantine. She drew back the curtains and looked down at the courtyard. A trail of scuffed and turned leaves traced from the door to the briar to the main gates and back. Had Alys been up already? She thought about sending the invisible ones down to clear the paths but it cost so much. She'd save them for the tasks Philippe would notice. He noticed less and less now.

She could see glossy new leaves decking every twig of the briar beside the garden gate. The gnarled trunk was smoothing into curves. Stout thorns studded every limb. Buds swelled at every tip. A promise of hope, of life. A pledge that her long years of guardianship would not be wasted. Philippe's power was waning as the curse progressed. One way or another, Eglantine would soon be free.

She could see a spot of red at the tip of one branch and longed to bury her face within the petals and breathe in the spice-sharp scent. A reminder of what never needed words.

"I love you too," she whispered and drew the curtains.

Grace lay down again on the bed and gathered her strength to send the invisible ones about their morning chores. The household must go on as usual. Philippe must not know her weakness. She would rise later and join them to dine.

ALYS WAS TROUBLED. SHE could see the girl's discomfort as they sat to dine in the parlor. Was it a passing melancholy? Or did she, too, sense the end drawing near? What would become of Alys? Would she make her way back home to her family again? Or would Philippe—finally quit of any last trace of pity—rend her limb from limb? How much time did they have? She watched Alys fidget with her dinner, staring at the roast capon as if she expected it to turn to serpents and strike. Perhaps it might. One could never tell with Philippe. No, not serpents. He couldn't transform life into death or death into life.

Alys gave a deep and shuddering breath and set her fork down on the plate with a clink. With eyes cast down she asked, "What became of Eglantine?"

The moment froze in time as Philippe's eyes narrowed and a hollow opened in Grace's chest. She remembered well the last time that question had been asked. *What's become of Eglantine?*

SHE HAD CALCULATED SO, so carefully when and how to ask. The horses had been stabled just as if she truly had returned from a journey. Half the day had passed with her nerves stretched thin as gossamer. She mustn't speak too soon or he'd hear suspicion. She mustn't wait too long or he'd be certain she already knew the answer.

"What's become of Eglantine?" A tone of confusion and curiosity, carefully crafted.

"Gone," Philippe had snapped. "Left without a word of thanks or farewell. The ungrateful bitch."

As the venom spewed from out his mouth, she must play concern, regret, bewilderment. Philippe must not know that she knew. He mustn't know they'd planned to leave together. Not while Eglantine was still within his power. Not when only he could bring her back.

He'd tire of the game. He'd relent, if not forgive. There'd be another chance. She had only to wait until Peronelle returned—an ally against Philippe's spite. The days passed and she waited. And waited.

She would speak of Eglantine now and again, reminding Philippe of her sweetness and her joy. Surely his mood would turn. But with every passing day he remembered only that Eglantine had refused him. That she had rejected his offer and sought to escape, though he never used that word.

Philippe must never know she knew. What excuse could she offer for having waited outside the gate in the dead of that night? Perhaps he suspected, but he didn't *know*. Knowledge would be a weapon in his hands. A weapon like the knife he sometimes toyed with while walking the garden paths: the sort of knife a gardener might use for removing errant branches or cutting pleachers for a hedge. Or cutting down briars. He would stare at the rose bush and finger the hilt of the knife. She would stand frozen in place until he moved on. Philippe must never know where her deepest weakness lay.

When Peronelle came, it would be time enough to speak. Peronelle could stand against him as she never could.

But then she came and Grace had no chance to warn her, to take her aside and explain. Philippe fed her lies and bile, raging against the woman who should have been his betrothed, calling her names so vile Grace couldn't bear to remember them. Complaining that she'd run off and God alone could find her.

Peronelle had turned, bewildered and angry, to Grace. "What has become of Eglantine?"

They were standing in the gardens. It had flowers then and bees buzzing and the scent of herbs. And by the wall where the little arched gate led out, a tangled briar, too wild to have known a gardener's hand. And Philippe standing there, trimming his nails with that sharp knife, grinning. In the space of a heartbeat, the deed could be done and Eglantine would be beyond saving with no proof of Philippe's guilt.

A lifetime's caution had shown her the path. Grace clutched her terror close inside and set her face to stillness and her voice to smooth and polished stone and said, "I do not know." And nothing more. Philippe must not know. Grace tried to signal to Peronelle, sending the invisible ones to tug about her clothing and draw her gaze to the garden gate. She didn't heed them. Instead, she raised her arms, and with a crack of lightning Grace felt herself caught frozen by the woman's power. Philippe stood suspended in the act of calling on his own glamours. In a voice dripping with anguish and love, Peronelle called a curse down on them.

"You, Philippe du Fortigny, are a beast! And you, Grace du Fortigny, are a creature of stone. These things you are. These things you will become unless you repent. I thought to entrust my treasure, the delight of my life, to you—you who know nothing of love. Not until you prove me wrong will the curse be broken. From this day forth until three days, three and thirty years are spent, if true love is offered and returned within these walls you will be free. If even that is beyond you, become what you deserve for all time!"

No! Grace wanted to shout. *She's here, she lives, she needs you!* But the paralysis of cowardice had been made manifest in her body. She saw Philippe's handsome form twist and contort, and felt her flesh beginning to chill and harden. Not until Peronelle opened the gates and took the path to other worlds were they released to move once more.

Their guests slipped away after her. No one would risk Peronelle's wrath by staying. By the end of the week their mortal servants had all fled. Philippe raised a glamour around Bettencourt to hide from fée and mortal alike and raged against the curse.

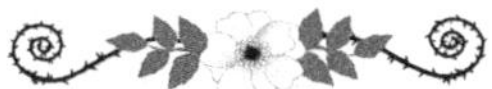

FOR NEARLY THREE AND thirty years she had waited, hoping that some girl who found her way to Bettencourt would catch Philippe's heart. If that failed, at least the triumph of the curse would free everything that had been caught up in Philippe's sorcery. But now, when no hope was left to her except in that silent waiting, must Alys stir it up again and bring disaster on them all?

"What has become of Eglantine?"

Philippe had turned from Alys to stare at her, seeing betrayal. Silence wouldn't serve this time—not as it had before. Who else could have told her?

"That's a name that hasn't been spoken in this house for many years," Grace said. "Did you find it written on the flyleaf of one of the books you catalogued? Eglantine might have left one or two behind after her visit." It was a plausible enough story.

Alys still stared at her plate. Her shoulders were tense as if waiting for a blow. Philippe's lips curled in a snarl. He gestured at the plates to dismiss the dinner. This time, the food wavered in substance to dry leaves and back before turning to muck.

Grace picked her way through the thorns, choosing her words with care. "Eglantine was the adopted daughter of Peronelle Latour, a woman of ancient name and a friend of our parents. There was a time everyone thought that Eglantine and Philippe might wed. But they didn't suit and she left."

"She just…left?" Alys asked, lifting her eyes to meet Grace's with suspicion and doubt.

"She—" Grace began.

"She was a whore," Philippe roared, slamming his hand down on the table and tearing at the cloth with his claws. "Smiling and teasing and promising herself to me. Then giving her smiles and kisses to another. She betrayed me."

He stared down along the length of the table directly at Grace.

He knew, she realized. Her heart froze. He had always known. Her silence, her caution, all the long years… She'd thought to protect them both from his malice with her silence, her pretended ignorance. But this had always been his revenge: the waiting itself, bound here by love and hope to suffer under his thumb. The years without Eglantine's face and voice before her. The absence of her touch. The torment as he pushed her deeper and deeper into that silence, thinking there was a way out. And now at the end, she had lost all reflex to do otherwise.

"Philippe was, of course, disappointed when she left," Grace said evenly. "Eglantine was a lovely young woman. And Peronelle Latour was a powerful sorceress. It would have been a good alliance." She kept talking, babbling, anything to stop Philippe's mouth and keep him from speaking that lurking truth.

Slowly the angry glint in his eye faded to self-pity. He reached out his paw to Alys in the customary invitation to the dance, though dinner was not half-finished. "Eglantine didn't have your biddable sweetness. You know how fortunate you are to have my love, even if you scorn it. Come, shall we dance?"

Grace gritted her teeth and sent the invisible ones to the harpsichord. For a time, the music filled the room and bodies moved in paths of habit through the small space until, with a crash, Alys stumbled against a chair left pulled out from the table and cried out as Philippe gripped her to keep her from falling.

"Why is the room in disarray?" he growled. "You see? You've stirred up memories that make me clumsy with your silly questions."

Alys had found her feet again but still he gripped her.

"Alys," came the low rumbling growl. "Do *you* love me? Will you marry me?"

Usually, the answer came softly with a tinge of sorrow. This time Alys's tongue seemed frozen in her mouth, until at last she managed, "N—no, Philippe."

He released her and pushed her away, making her stagger to keep her balance. "Good night to the both of you," he spat out.

In that moment, Grace knew what had to be done.

 The Fugitive

THE DREAM THAT WOKE me was more confusing than any before. Lady Rose had been there—the rose was present in all my dreams now, petals framing her worried face—but Father was there as well. He reached for a rose—no, for Lady Rose, her skin the green-brown of bark, rough with ridges and leaf-scars. Or was it Philippe who was grasping the rose? They shifted in that way of dreams. When I tried to ask Lady Rose what was happening, she spoke in words for the first time, "Hold me tight. Don't let me go."

So I held tightly to the thorny stem, to the bark-skinned woman. Under my fingers, the bark shredded and began sloughing off and she slipped away. I cried out, fearing that I'd hurt her. Someone was holding me back, pulling at my garments, tugging me awake.

I opened my eyes with my heart pounding from the feel of hands on me until I recognized the touch of Grace's unseen servants. The room was dark. The glow of moonlight that had broken through the night before was again shrouded behind clouds. The hands tugged at me again, insistent and demanding. I sat up, whispering, "What is it? What do you want?" I didn't expect a reply—they had never spoken aloud. And having roused me, now they let me be.

Something was wrong. I fumbled for slippers and found a dressing gown laid out across a chair. The rose was still in my hand, reminding me of that command, *Hold me tight. Don't let me go.* As I pulled the dressing gown around me, I tucked the rose into one wide sleeve where the thorns snagged on the lining to hold it hidden.

The corridor was lit faintly by one distant candle, and the unseen servants guided me by soft touches to the stairs and down. Questions chased through my mind. The night before, Lady Rose had woken me and sent me out into the moonlight. Who called this time? Had the woman from the wood found her way within the manor's sorceries? Was she commanding the invisible servants?

From the foot of the staircase, I could see a glow spilling out the open door of the parlor and the touch of the invisible ones ceased as I approached. Grace sat in her usual place at one end of the long dining table. Not slumped over in sleep this time, but sitting stiffly erect. She laid a finger to her lips in caution when she saw me and beckoned me close. In a voice barely more than a whisper, she said, "I'm sending you home."

Yesterday's doubts dissolved in confusion once more. Could I trust her, or was this another deceit? Had the woman in the wood lied to me from the first? Perhaps Eglantine had simply left as Grace had said.

"Grace, what about—?"

She stopped me with another shushing gesture.

"The time approaches. There's nothing more that you can do here. I can't protect you any-more." She stopped abruptly when she would have said more.

There was the faintest of creaks and Grace's eyes flew upward in the direction of Philippe's chamber, but it was no more than the building settling in the night.

"Philippe must not know until you are well quit of this place," Grace continued. "He can't change you unless he can see you. His power is fading but he could still do you harm. In the stable is an old palanquin. Close yourself within it and don't open the door until you know your-self to be home. I've greased the hinges on the garden gate and swept the dry leaves from the paths. There should be no sound of your going until you're well away."

There was no space in Grace's instructions for me to protest or refuse. Fear shone through from her normally serene and expressionless face.

"What about you?" I began.

Grace shook her head. "In a fortnight, the term of the curse will be complete. And when Philippe is entirely the beast and I am motionless stone, what will become of you? There's nothing you can do for me now."

And—heaven forgive me—I took her at her word.

I slipped out the great front doors as I had the night before and made my way around to where the stable doors stood open. In the space between the stalls, a palanquin stood waiting. A grand sedan chair like those Father had described seeing in Paris, with carved and gilded wood on the frame and silk brocade covering the cushioned seats and curtaining the windows. The silk was dusty and stained with age and the gilding on the wood was peeling. The glamour of Bettencourt had not touched it. Two long poles lay to either side, waiting for the chair men to lift them into place. But there were no chair men of course, except for…the near door of the palanquin swung open invitingly. Grace's unseen servants, of course.

I stepped up into the seat and settled myself as the door closed and latched behind me. With barely a jostle, I felt the palanquin being lifted from the ground. It moved with unearthly smoothness. I wouldn't even have known when we left the grounds except for the slight *snick* of the gate latch.

CHAPTER TWENTY-TWO

THE GUARDIAN

IN THE PARLOR, GRACE sat motionless. Her bones burned with fire as she poured all her power into the invisible ones on their journey. Looking through their eyes, she could see the palanquin speeding through the night along the tree-lined road. Before dawn, they came to the village and the house of the merchant Levesque. When they had set the palanquin gently on the cobbled yard, she called them back and gathered them about her.

Now came the final siege. The vigil that would give meaning to all these years. Slowly, Grace rose to her feet and moved through the hall, out the door, and down the garden path to where the briar climbed beside the gate. She braced her feet to stand firm—the encroaching stone in her flesh would only aid her now—and gently wrapped her arms around the briar, caressing the curves of the knotted trunk. The thorns gave no pain. Around her a wealth of swollen buds were waiting for release.

Grace set the invisible ones around them in a ring. A wall that would stand impenetrable so long as her strength held. And then she waited. And waited.

CHAPTER TWENTY-THREE

THE PRODIGAL

ANTON WAS WOKEN BY the housekeeper's knock and a soft "Monsieur Levesque, you must come down."

He grunted and would have rolled back to sleep but Madame Sauvin stood stubbornly at his bedside holding out a dressing gown.

"Monsieur, it's the strangest thing. You must come down."

He stumbled down the stairs to the front door where the servants were all gathered staring into the yard. There, in the pale dawn, stood a gilded palanquin furnished in faded brocade, with no sign of footmen or carriers, as out of place on the cobbles as a peacock would have been in his stable.

"Is this some joke?" Anton asked of no one in particular. "Where did it come from?"

"No one knows," Madame Sauvin answered. "Constance saw it when she went out to gather eggs."

Anton straightened his clothing and assumed a forbidding expression before he descended to approach the arrival. The palanquin rocked slightly and the door handle turned, then swung open. There, wearing night clothes and rubbing her sleep-muddled eyes, was his eldest daughter.

"Alys?" he asked, in bewilderment.

In the moment before she rushed into his arms, Anton couldn't have said what he felt. Relief? Joy? Dread? He had made his peace with her fate—or what he imagined that fate might be. In the past two years life had settled into new, more prosperous patterns and his lost daughter had become a story, told and embellished over glasses of wine in the evenings. And now here she was, unannounced, disheveled like a runaway bride, and very much alive.

"Father!" Alys cried. "Oh Father, I'm back!"

Anton wrapped his arms around her, murmuring, "My child, my dear child." He felt a sharp stab in his arm like a pang of memory and pushed her away. "What's this?"

It was a rose. A deep pink rose on a sturdy thorny stem.

"I hope you haven't been stealing enchanted roses!" he chided with an uneasy laugh and reached to take it from her. "We might have this to do all over again."

Alys pulled the flower back, away from his grasp. "No, Father," she said. "It's the same rose—the one you picked. The one I was sent to redeem. There's no further debt to pay for it."

That was impossible, of course. He'd have the real story, but not yet.

"Sauvin," he ordered, "go tell my daughters their sister has returned to us."

ANTON HADN'T NOTICED HOW quiet and empty the house had become until it was filled again with the chatter of women. Quick steps crossed the floor above, back and forth, as Henriette and Louise-Marie set to work tidying their sister and finding garments for her. Alys's old clothing had been made over or given away. And her old things wouldn't have been suitable for the sister of Henriette d'Antras and Louise-Marie

Corneille, who were now among the foremost ladies of the town.

Why had she returned? Anton was impatient for the answer, though he knew it would come more easily in the dressing room upstairs than under his questioning. But when Henriette came down to send Constance off to fetch powder and scent, she only shook her head and said Alys promised to tell all over dinner. Dinner—when his sons-in-law would be present and there would be no chance to quietly overlook disaster. Was there anything Alys could explain that wouldn't be considered disaster, given how she had arrived?

Jean-Claude Corneille and Pierre d'Antras knew the story, of course. He'd told it often enough over the past two years. And when they were all seated about the dining table and the soup had been served, he launched into it one more time, embellished at great length with descriptions of the echoing manor house and the invisible servants and the monster in the garden. They knew, of course, about the treasure he'd brought back. At the opposite end of the table, Alys sat quietly, eating with an odd hesitancy as if it had been long since she'd seen good food. What had they done to her in all that time?

He took the story up to their farewell and then the return of his horse, days later, found in its stable one morning with saddle and bridle hung where they belonged. "And now, Alys, tell us what you found there. How have you fared all this time?"

"Has it been two years?" she asked. "I wasn't sure. Bettencourt was a strange place. Outside the walls, the seasons changed, but within it seemed eternal autumn. Nothing but dry dead leaves came past the walls unless Lord Philippe allowed otherwise. The rooms that Lord Philippe and Lady Grace occupied were grandly furnished, but—"

"Who is Lord Philippe?" Anton interrupted.

Alys set her spoon aside and would not meet his eyes. "The owner of the manor. The beast."

"Ah, then Lady Grace is the pale lady, I suppose. His wife."

"His sister," Alys said.

Anton frowned and adjusted his suspicions. If Alys would only get on with the matter, he wouldn't have to guess at things. He'd told the story so often about the beast-man and his marble-skinned wife and now he'd look a fool to have it contradicted.

"The rooms we occupied were sumptuous," Alys continued slowly. "But if you turned a corridor or went up a disused stair you might find peeling plaster and bare floors. There were no servants except the invisible ones, but they saw to our every need. And Lord Philippe provided the rest by sorcery."

It wasn't the story Anton had expected. The others were rapt, listening to Alys's description of her first day at Bettencourt: the fine bedchamber, the strange dinner, the invisible musicians playing for the dance.

"And then Lord Philippe asked if I loved him and if I'd marry him."

Anton felt his worries melt away. So she hadn't returned to them compromised and ruined. But then why—?

Louise-Marie gave a happy sigh. "To marry him! A grand lord with a manor house."

But Alys looked down at her plate. "He asked me if I loved him, so of course I said no."

Henriette frowned a little. "Love's a grand thing," she said and patted her husband's hand where it lay on the table beside hers. "But a lord…oh, Alys, just think of it!"

"Go on, go on," Anton urged. "And then what?"

Alys had always kept her own council. He'd liked that. Women shouldn't always be badgering a man with chatter and advice, especially not daughters. But didn't she see that he needed to know everything? He watched her mouth work, as if she were choosing and discarding stories.

"Every day after that was much the same," Alys said. "I would go walking in the empty gardens in the morning and do what chores I could find in the afternoon. Lord Philippe would come and try to amuse me sometimes, and Lady Grace often shared my morning walks. We'd dine together, and every night Lord Philippe would lead me in the dance and ask me if I loved him. But I never did, so I always said no. And so they sent me home. Father, I'm sorry, I'm just tired. I'll tell you more tomorrow."

"Then you aren't married," Anton asked with sinking heart.

"No, Father."

ONE DAY WAS THE most Anton was willing to give her to rest. One day to imagine the worst and wonder how it could be remedied. When they sat together for dinner the next day, just the two of them this time, he sent the servants away.

"No more secrets," he said. "More than a year in that place and all you can tell us is that you walked in the garden and had dinner and danced?"

"The days were so much alike, one to the other. I scarcely know what to tell."

So that was the game she meant to play. "I have been thinking, Alys, that you should reconsider."

She looked up with a mock-innocent expression. "Reconsider what?"

"I mean that however ugly this Lord Philippe might be—and I acknowledge that his visage was quite terrifying—an offer of marriage from a lord is nothing to dismiss lightly, however peculiar his life might be."

"It's too late for that," she said.

"It's too late to think matters can go on as they were!" Anton reined in his impatience. "If you go back and beg his forgiveness, surely a man who could propose to you night after night for two years would consider doing so again. You need to consider your future. Our future."

Alys shook her head. "No, Father, it's too late for me to break the curse. It's nearly run its course. That's why I left."

"You could have broken the curse by marrying him?" Anton struggled to remember the scraps he'd overheard that strange night. It was easier to remember the stories he'd turned them into.

"No, Father," she said. "I could have broken the curse if I loved him."

"Love," Anton said bitterly. "You couldn't manage to love him even to have all that? You broke his heart and left him and for what? Because you wanted a child's dream of love. Just like your mother."

Alys looked up at him, and for a moment, Anton was reminded of his long-departed wife. Not in her face, but in that quiet stubbornness that refused to bend or compromise.

"I've dreamed about her sometimes," Alys said. "Did she leave because you didn't love her?"

How could she ask such a question? How could she doubt him?

"Your mother was beautiful—so beautiful. I would have given her the moon and the stars. Everything I had was hers. I promised her anything she asked. And she twisted my promises into traps. Nothing I could do was good enough for her. And so she betrayed me and left. Never question whether I loved her! Aren't you proof enough of that?"

His voice was shaking and he found himself standing over Alys, daring her to challenge him. But that echo of defiance drained away and she shrank back. Did she fear he would strike her? What had they done at Bettencourt to steal his cheerful, obedient daughter?

"Alys," he began, coaxingly, "surely—" She shook her head and looked away. He gave a loud sigh and left her standing there. She would come to understand. He wanted what was best for her, and what could be better than a noble marriage? There was still time; there must be.

THE KEY

OH, MY SUN, MY sun! What have you done? She was our hope and you sent her away. I can barely reach her now across the miles, even though the mist is fading. I come to her in dreams to beg her aid but I can only speak in pearls and roses across the miles.

What is it, Lady Rose? she asks. *What must I do?*

I take her hand to lead her back and it slips through my fingers and I fumble for her in the dark. *Don't leave us,* I want to say. *Come back to us!* Even if I could speak in words, what I would say? There must be a reason she heard my call, a reason she came in answer to the rose. She must be the key, that's all I know.

Oh my sun, I won't abandon hope. Not while you still shine. I'll beg with all my strength and pray we aren't too late.

CHAPTER TWENTY-FIVE

THE BETRAYER

Lady Rose came into my dreams again that night, pleading with wide dark eyes, but when she tried to speak, pearls fell from her mouth. When I woke, my rose had turned the dull, leaden purple that I remembered meant fear. Even as I held it, the aroma faded—not a rose's scent but one that reminded me of forget-me-nots in the evening chill.

Did I want to forget the years at Bettencourt? I'd be happy to lose the dread of seeing Philippe around every corner, but not Grace. I thought of Grace in every moment: how she had been like her invisible servants, always quietly present, always with comfort in their touch. Had she truly betrayed me from the start? But then why send me away? Would I have consented to go if the woman in the wood hadn't planted that seed of doubt?

When I looked at my rose more closely, I could see that the edges of the petals were dry and brown—just the faintest rim of blight. All this time she'd remained fresh and alive. Was she, too, touched by the curse? But the briar in the garden had seemed to be quickening even as Philippe sank deeper into the beast and Grace's movements slowed. I set the flower down on my dressing table, fearing it would crumble if I hid it under my pillow. Constance had been strictly instructed to let it be.

I spent that morning with Madame Sauvin reviewing the household accounts. Pierre d'Antras handled much of the business now, though I expected that it was Henriette whose word held sway. I'd managed our father's personal affairs before I left. Now he'd let them fall into a muddle.

"I'm glad you're back, Madame Alys," the housekeeper told me as she returned the keys to the household. "You've always known how to coax the master out of his moods, which is a knack I've never had. He wears me out."

It was good to feel useful once more. To be on my own ground. But I dreaded facing him over dinner again. Philippe had ground away the edges of the old Alys. Where once I would have softened Father with humor and cleared away the day's irritations, now I shrank within myself to wait out the storm. *Never question whether I loved her!* I'd never questioned that Philippe felt…something. But that hadn't been enough. Had it been enough for her?

"You knew my mother, didn't you?" I asked Madame Sauvin. I couldn't remember when she had come to our household. Had it been before or after?

She looked uncomfortable and said, "You know your father doesn't like to talk about her."

And yet he had. He'd invoked her to try to send me back to Bettencourt. "Did she love him?"

The housekeeper thought a while, then slowly said, "Your father adored her. He worshipped her. He couldn't believe his luck that a woman as beautiful and graceful as she was would smile at him."

"What happened?"

She fell silent for a bit and I waited, fearing that if I prodded, she would say no more.

"She was lovely, you know. Not just beautiful, but in a way that drew the eyes and caught your heart. So lovely that no one thought to ask where she had come from or who her people were. She was melancholy at first, but when your father began to court her, she bloomed like a garden. Just like in all the old stories. Your father promised her anything if only she'd marry him."

Yes, that sounded like Father. He was quick with a promise.

"Your mother…she had some odd notions. She said yes, but she made him swear three things. There were always to be cut flowers in the house, even in winter. That's why he built the summerhouse on the south side of the stable."

I thought about the small shed with all its expensive glass windows. I couldn't remember it being used for anything but storage.

"Everyone thought it so very romantic. She made him promise to leave the baptism of the children to her. Well, that was very odd, and though he promised, I know for a fact he took you all to the priest, though he never told her about it. What she didn't know wouldn't hurt her, he said."

Yes, that sounded like Father, too. When he knew what he was doing was right, he never questioned it. But Madame Sauvin was silent for a long time until I asked, "And the third promise?"

"The third promise was that he wasn't to lay a hand on her. I don't mean not touch her, but not to strike her. Such a notion! How could she even think it? But I remember at the wedding feast, the men were joking in the way men do about how soon he'd have sons. And your father turned to her and patted her on the cheek and said, 'They'll come soon enough,' and she went all still and said, 'That's one.' He was angry because she'd shamed him right there at the wedding. But he never struck her, I'll swear to that!"

"Was that why she left?" I asked. Had the tragedy turned on such a small twist of meaning? To pat her cheek and have her treat it as a blow? Surely, he hadn't intended…

Madame Sauvin nodded. "I never saw the second time. But when Louise-Marie was born—I was there you see, holding the babe so your mother could rest. Your father…he always wanted sons. A man does, you know. He sat on the bedside and told her they'd try again. She said that she had three flowers in her garden and that was enough. He took her by the shoulders—that was all, just holding her like that—and said of course they'd try again. And she said, 'That's three,' and then something like 'it's done,' or 'it's finished.'

"Well, at first, we all thought she was talking about her daughters, about you all. That she was finished having children. And three should surely be enough, though it would have been nice to have a boy around the house. But she disappeared that night and none of us saw her go. Maybe she said something more to your father because he was raging all the next day about how she'd lied and said he'd struck her. But none of us could believe that she'd leave her darling daughters behind for such a little thing as that."

She looked quickly toward the hall, as if worried that Father might have heard.

Such a little thing, I thought. A man's word. "I always thought it was us," I said quietly. "When Father would say she'd left because three daughters was too much, I thought it was our fault."

"You tried so hard, but you were seven years old. There was no telling you differently. You thought you had to take her place, but it was never your fault."

This time it *was* my fault. This time I was the one who had left. Did it matter that there was nothing I could have done for Grace? I'd still abandoned her.

MY FATHER'S HOUSE WAS solid in a way that Bettencourt had never been, but it felt emptier somehow. I thought at first it was only the absence of my sisters. They had their husbands. Louise-Marie had a child and another to come. They had set out on their own journeys and I had been left behind. But there was another lack. I felt it like the slow fading of Lady Rose with every dawn. Bettencourt's sorceries had been terrifying more often than not, but they had seeped under my skin. The world was thinner now without them. Soon there would be nothing left except the crumbled dust of petals and years stretching out before me as my father's companion.

Henriette had set herself the task of changing my mind where our father had failed.

"It won't do, you know," she confided once more as we walked slowly through town, back from shopping for laces and ribbons for my new gown. "People won't forget. It would be easier for us all if you went back and accepted Lord Philippe's offer. We could set it about that you'd only wanted to come back for a visit before the betrothal."

"And what of the curse?" I asked. "What of the curse that can only be broken by love?"

She took me by the arm and pulled me close. "Do you think love is all roses and sweetmeats? Love is putting someone else's happiness before your own."

Did she think I hadn't done that? All my life I'd put her happiness and Louise-Marie's before mine. When Father had stolen the rose from Bettencourt, I'd sacrificed myself for all of them when I thought it truly was a sacrifice. And now I was to put Philippe's desires first. When had anyone ever put *my* happiness before their own? No one…except for Grace, I thought.

Every curse must have its key. Had I been looking at the wrong lock? I'd thought only of Philippe: of husbands and wives. With Grace there had been shared comfort and quiet alliance. There had been more kindness in one morning spent with her on a garden bench than in all of Philippe's magical banquets. If she had conspired to bring me to Bettencourt, she'd never pressed me after that. She'd never demanded any answer but what I was willing to give. In the end, Grace had given her last hope of escape to open the cage for me. What was I willing to sacrifice for her in return? Had the answer been before me all this time? The realization struck me to the heart.

Henriette must have seen the change in my face. "Yes, you see?"

I didn't care that she'd misunderstood. That Father would think he'd convinced me. "I need to go back," I said and quickened my pace.

Father eagerly ordered the servants to drag the gilded palanquin out into the yard. It would carry me back, I was certain. All I needed to do was ask. That was how things worked at Bettencourt. When evening fell, I put on my new gown and carefully carried the faded rose in my hand—the petals nearly all lost now—and settled myself on the cushions.

"Take me back to Bettencourt, please," I asked. And then I waited.

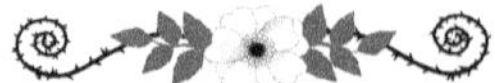

I WOULD HAVE SWORN THAT sleep was impossible, but I dreamed. I wandered lost in a forest without even Lady Rose at my side, only a dead, dry stem clutched in my fingers. The petals had all fallen but in their place the twig swelled into a scarlet hip. There was somewhere I must be but I couldn't find the way. In the shadows, a flash of white caught my eye: snowdrops out of season. A sign of hope. Another bit of color, this time heliotrope blue. That was for faithful devotion. Farther on, a spray of lily of the valley to mark a happy return. In my dream, each meaning was clear with no need for a book to guide me. I felt a sharp pain and looked down to find a thorn had pierced my thumb. Blood welled around it and I woke with a start.

A faint light seeped around the curtains of the motionless palanquin. With a sinking heart, I opened the door to find myself still in my father's courtyard. My hand throbbed in pain but instead of a withered rose, I held a small wooden key, smeared on the edges with blood though no wound could be seen. There was no time to wonder. I tucked the key within my bosom and went to pound on the stable door to wake the sleeping grooms.

"Still here, Mademoiselle Alys?" one said with a sleepy grin.

"Saddle my father's horse," I ordered, trying to turn the urgent panic in my voice to calm authority.

Memory guided me for the first part of the journey, and as the woods closed in around me, I knew what to look for. A patch of snowdrops. A trail of violets. At first the flowers appeared barely at the edges of my vision, but as the day passed from morn to noon, more sprang up, edging my path until a carpet of flowers led me to the clearing before the gates of Bettencourt as the sun began to dim.

CHAPTER TWENTY-SIX

THE SENTINEL

Y OU WATCHED HER GO, didn't you, Peronelle? You heard the gate swing open and saw a glimpse of the barren courtyard as the palanquin emerged before the gate and the glamour closed in again. You watched the invisible ones carry the girl away from Bettencourt and your heart surged in triumph that their last chance of rescue was gone. Don't deny it, Peronelle. You never wanted the curse to be broken, you wanted your revenge.

You didn't stay to witness those last days yourself, did you Peronelle? You left your spies in place to warn you of any change, but you didn't stay to hear Philippe's howls as the beast took final hold. You didn't peer through the bars as the glamour tore and wavered to see the invisible ones encircle Grace in a fragile armor. You didn't hear the clink of teeth on almost-stone or smell the blood from thorn-ripped flesh. You would return at the end to claim your triumph. That would be enough, wouldn't it, Peronelle?

But then the girl returned. You spies told you and you sped to the gates of Bettencourt to warn her off, lest your victory be snatched away.

You stood there in the clearing before the manor and watched the exhausted horse stumble through the dusk. When the girl slipped from its back you stepped out to block her way and told her, "It's too late. You cannot save them."

She didn't listen, did she, Peronelle? What did you see in her eyes? Did you see an echo of your own determination? The surety that she would see justice done?

She pushed past you to rattle the bars of the broad iron gates. There were no unseen hands to open them to her this time.

She turned to beg you, "Help me."

You could have done so, Peronelle. Philippe's power was nearly gone and yours could be turned to use. You could have commanded the trees to uproot the walls. But you shook your head in mock regret and asked, "Do you have a key?"

She jerked as if pricked by a thorn and reached within her bosom to pull out a small carved wand. And you thought, *Surely it will break in the lock. Surely, I won't be thwarted this close to the end.*

But it didn't break, did it, Peronelle? It turned, and the gate groaned and swung open. You could feel the last traces of Philippe's glamour as you passed within, like cobwebs trying to block your passage. Within those walls you could see Bettencourt as it truly was now. You could see the crumbling stones, the rotted doors, the flap of ragged curtains at the broken windows.

How long did it take you to turn your gaze to the statue in the yard? What did you see there? Did you begin to doubt, or were you still as blinkered as you had ever been? Let me tell you what you should have seen. A marble statue of a cloaked woman, her arms raised and her beautiful face contorted in struggle. The stone of the cloak was rent in sculpted tatters and stained with streaks of brownish red. And around that marble, a briar twined, wrapping it in thick loops, studded everywhere with thorns. Every branch of the briar was swollen with buds and new leaves, and the thorns turned outward at every point, a fence protecting what lay within.

And from somewhere within the manor, a beast howled.

 THE THORN

LADY ROSE HAD GIVEN me the key and marked out my path—I was certain it had been her—but no one could tell me what must be done next. No use to ask the woman from the wood, I knew that now. Grace stood motionless in struggle. I could only hope that life still hid within the stone. And beside her... I knew that Lady Rose was bound in some way to the briar. Now I saw that the thorny vines and the woman in my dreams were one. As if tossed by a wind, her branching arms encircled Grace. I thought of the enchanted popinjay and every careless transformation Philippe had performed for me. I could have guessed the whole story in that moment, but there was no time.

"Philippe!" I shouted.

Another howl answered me. Louder this time.

He emerged from the broken doorway of the manor, like and unlike the Philippe du Fortigny that I'd left a week past. He walked on all fours now, with a shape that spoke of wolf and bear. Only shreds of his fine clothing hung about his limbs and his dark fur was matted with blood and filth.

"Philippe," I called with less confidence and walked forward with my hand out, as if he were a strange dog.

He snarled and stalked stiff-legged, circling around me, as a wolf might its prey.

My voice shook as I solemnly proclaimed, "Philippe du Fortigny, I will marry you."

He lifted his head and howled and a shiver ran through me. I thought it was fear, but in the same moment he wavered in my sight. And then he charged, but not at me. Philippe circled the statue of his sister, as if it were a treasure he protected, and growled, "Mine! Mine! She's mine!"

I called out desperately, "Philippe!" What were the words I needed? "Philippe, do you hear me? I'll marry you!"

"Mine!" he cried once more and leapt to bite at Grace's outstretched arms.

The wind caught up a limb of the briar and dashed it against his muzzle. He yelped in pain and backed off a step. No, it couldn't be the wind—the air in the courtyard was still. Nor was it the invisible ones, protecting their mistress. As I watched, the briar's trunk twisted and split into two thick legs, pulling long-rooted feet free of the ground. It stepped toward Philippe where he crouched. Branches thick with thorns and buds swung around and whipped at him, sending him yelping backwards two more steps.

"Mine," he whined in confusion and surprise. Did his voice sound more like a man's now?

The thorny arms ripped at him, leaving bloody streaks across his fur. He tried to flee but a branch lashed out and wrapped around one leg. As he writhed on the ground, the briar-woman gave him stroke after relentless stroke. The canes tore long strips of skin and flesh from his limbs. The terrible cries slowly quieted to a low whimper, barely more than the sound of pained breathing. And then he lay still.

With a crack like the breaking of a branch, a mouth opened on the briar's trunk and in a rasping voice it said, "My own, Philippe. Never yours. My *own*." With a slow movement of trailing roots, the briar turned back toward Grace.

I went to crouch at Philippe's side, listening to his faint panting. Need I say it once more? But his shattered body shifted, in that way of death, from mere stillness to emptiness. Had I been in time?

The woman from the wood was there beside me. Her words dripped with scorn. "Foolish girl! You never loved him. Did you think you could cheat my curse?"

I stood, clenching my hands into fists. "I didn't come back for him! I came for her!"

We both turned in time to see Grace slump to the ground, her flesh soft and supple once more. Arms caught her as she fell. Lithe, thick-muscled arms that shed strands of bark. Rooted trunks became strong, rounded legs. Twigs and branches twisted into a riot of mahogany curls as every bud burst in a crown of dark crimson petals and fell in a shower about her feet. The crack of a mouth called to itself lips and cheeks and flashing eyes.

And at my side, the woman from the wood, in a voice of anguished recognition, whispered, "Eglantine!"

The Changeling

OH, MY LOVE, MY sunshine, my dear one! How long you waited! How faithfully you watched! So close I came to losing you forever!

I gathered you senseless in my arms and would have been content to remain so, but I could not bear to be near *him*. I lifted you—you who had been ponderous stone a moment before and now felt lighter than a leaf.

I heard my name being called, but I wasn't ready to speak to her. Did you understand yet what you'd done, Peronelle? What you'd failed to see?

I gazed at the crumbling ruin that was Bettencourt and wondered if it could offer shelter. If I could bear to enter it with *him* still there, a heap of flesh in the shape of a man.

"Lady Rose?" It was the girl. The one I'd spoken to in dreams. "Lady Rose, there is a cottage—a woodcutter's home—it isn't far. We don't need to stay here."

I followed her out through the gates where her horse stood waiting. You stirred, but I wouldn't surrender you. Not yet. It was not so far and you weren't heavy. Not anymore.

Peronelle followed us silently.

The girl, Alys, was the one who thought of small, practical things. As I laid you in the narrow bed, unwilling to leave your side, she found kindling to start a fire, and fetched water, and from somewhere found a cookpot and the makings of porridge. A plain, human food with nothing of sorcery. When was the last time you'd eaten, my love? How many days had you stood guard over me in the garden at the end?

Alys brought a bowl and spoon and set it in my hands, saying, "See that she eats it all."

"Thank you," I said. A bright, peach-pink blossom fell from my lips with the words and I laughed to see it fall. "I had forgotten." A pearl followed the flower and rolled across the floor.

Between mouthfuls of the porridge, Grace beckoned the girl over and reached to clasp her hand, saying, "Alys, you came back."

The girl blushed and nodded. "Lady Rose showed me the way."

"Lady Rose?"

She looked over at me. "Lady Eglantine, I mean. But I didn't know her name, only that she was my rose." And then, as if she'd thought better of it, "Not *my* rose of course, but my friend who was a rose."

And then she turned away in confusion, her face full of more questions than she knew how to ask. For so long I'd called to her, coaxed her, and begged her. She'd whispered her fears and secrets to me, but I knew so little of her heart. Only that she had been willing to marry *him* for Grace's sake. For that, I would be ever in her debt.

When she'd set out more food on the small table, Alys picked up a lantern and said, "I'm going to the manor to fetch some things—if there's anything left now that Philippe's magic has gone. Is there anything you want?"

"Don't trouble yourself for me," Grace said. "There will be plenty of time to sort through what remains."

"Do you mean to stay, then?" I asked as Alys slipped out the door. Tiny spikes of pink betony flowers followed the words. Betony for surprise. I'd need to relearn how to lie in flowers.

"It's my inheritance. There is a deep magic in that place, gathered down the years. But if you say the word, I'll wander the ends of the earth penniless with you instead."

"I had wondered—" Peronelle began.

I hadn't forgotten she was there, but I hadn't yet brought myself to speak to her.

"I had wondered if you both might return with me to Tourdespine."

Now I rose and turned, the despair of three and thirty years welling in my throat. Thorns tore at my tongue and blood spattered the marigolds that fell from my lips. "You never saw me. You never saw *me*. Oh, Peronelle, you pride yourself on seeing things as they are. On shaping things as you see them."

I'd never dared to tell her these things the last time I'd had speech. She was the great Peronelle Latour and I was what she had shaped me to be.

"You thought that for me to love you I must cease to love my parents. You thought a child must either be yours entirely or nothing at all. You thought that a man could either be charming or a beast and not both. You thought I should love Philippe du Fortigny but you never thought I might love Grace. You thought cold only came from lack of care and not from caring too much."

I was weeping pearls now, not from the pain of the thorns but from all those long years of not being *seen*.

"You never knew my heart, so when Philippe changed my skin, you couldn't recognize me. And now you ask me to return with you to Tourdespine, to be tended in your garden and pruned and clipped back to your loving daughter."

There was no need for me to give any other answer. Peronelle bowed her head and went out into the darkening yard. I didn't care whether she returned or not.

 The Sisters

ETTENCOURT HAD THE LOOK of an old ruin now. Whatever parts Philippe had enchanted into good repair and splendor had returned to what the hand of man had built and the touch of time and nature had worn down. Here and there was a bit of old elegance: the harpsichord still stood in the parlor, though the notes jangled untunefully now. The library still held books, though not so many as I had catalogued. But most of the rooms resembled what I'd seen those times I turned an unexpected corner to a place Philippe had no use for.

I had little hope of finding food in the kitchens. All of Philippe's enchantments had died with him. I thought suddenly of the gold that had been Louise-Marie's dowry and wondered whose hands it had passed into by now. The corners of an empty bin turned up a handful of shriveled barley grains, and the remains of a sack held a few dried peas. Perhaps magic had kept the mice away. I tucked them away in the pocket under my skirts.

Clothing and blankets were my next thought. Lady Eglantine would need something to wear. We were nearly of a size and perhaps my old traveling dress had been left behind when the transformations failed.

I climbed the staircase, holding the lantern high and taking care for rotted boards. In the chamber that had been my own, there were bits of old furniture tossed about and smashed. No doubt Philippe had spent his anger here when he found me gone. The bedding was still whole. Good linen will last forever and the same magic that banished mice had kept the blankets free of moths. And there, beneath the cloth, was the small green book that had been hidden under my pillow. It had been trodden underfoot but no pages were torn. I smoothed the covers and put it in my pocket along with the grain.

There was only a sliver of moon when I stepped out into the courtyard but no mist to hide it now and I could still see the outlines of the manor even in full dark. Did Grace really mean to live here? But home was home. Perhaps she had good memories here that could wash away those lost years. Memories like being held close in a pair of arms and a voice singing a lullaby? I'd kept those safe against the passing of the years. They could build new memories. Would Eglantine consent to live in a place that surely held only pain and terror for her? Perhaps. There was a deep contentment between the two of them and an understanding that three and thirty years of waiting had only deepened. And they were fée with many years to come.

And what of me? I couldn't go back to live in my father's house. No one would believe a story about betrothal now. I'd be ruined—we all would be. Love is putting someone else's happiness before your own. I truly had been willing to be married to Philippe for Grace's sake. Compared to that, could I make the smaller sacrifice of leaving my family in peace?

That could wait. There were more practical matters to manage now. Food, fire, comforts. I enjoyed providing those. There was the joke: I would have made someone a good wife, if not for the matter of being a wife. Perhaps that was a way to make my living somewhere, in a city where no one knew my name.

MADAME LATOUR WAS SITTING on a rough log bench outside the cottage door and rose to come meet me, as if she didn't want those inside to know she was still there. As the cloaked woman in the woods, she'd been frightening. Now she scarcely seemed a fée at all, only a tired old woman. She stared at me curiously, as if I were a puzzle to solve.

"Madame Latour," I said. I put my bundle down and curtseyed to her, if only to break that gaze.

"They called you Alys," she said hesitantly. "I had…I knew…there was a girl, perhaps your age, named Alys. Alys…?"

"Alys Levesque," I supplied.

She drew in her breath, but not in surprise, I thought.

"So I haven't lost everyone. I still have you."

Her words made no sense. Then suddenly she took me in an embrace and I was surrounded by the spicy-sweet scent of roses. I knew that scent: a voice, a song, arms rocking me softly.

I broke free and stepped back. Silence settled in around us so deeply I could hear the soft whicker of my father's horse in the woodcutter's shed. My tongue froze in my mouth.

When an age had passed and still I'd said nothing, she continued, "He broke the rules. Your father. He promised, then he broke his word. I couldn't stay."

She searched my face, looking for something.

The years swirled around me like pieces of a puzzle that fell into new places.

"Let me give you those years back," she said. "Let me offer you a home. Be my daughter once more. Let me make amends."

I couldn't think. I couldn't breathe. I didn't know what to say, so I said something foolish. "If you want to make amends, you might conjure up some supper."

She blinked in surprise.

"There was almost nothing in the woodcutter's stores. Everything we ate at Bettencourt came from Philippe's sorcery. It's two days' ride to town and back. There may be some withered apples on the trees but that's all."

Madame Latour shook her head slowly. "I can't conjure food from nothing as Philippe du

Fortigny could. My power is to help things to what they truly are."

"That's not true!" I said hotly. "Grace was never ice and stone!"

She closed her eyes and bowed her head. It was enough of an admission. "If there were seeds…"

I reached through my skirt to the pocket and scooped out the handful of withered barley and dried peas and offered it to her. She took the seeds and cast them out across the yard, then raised her arms. In the flickering light of the lantern, I saw green blades spring up. Tendrils of pea shoots twined up dry stalks of mullein. Leaves spread and flowers bloomed even there in the dark. Grain swelled on nodding stems and peas in their pods. It was enough to keep us for a week, though not in dainty splendor, with fodder for the horse besides. "Thank you," I said.

She helped me gather some of the harvest into my skirt and ventured once more, "Will you come? Will you be my daughter once more?"

"I had a mother once," I replied. I flinched from how cold my voice sounded. "She left when my youngest sister was still in the cradle. When I was a child, I needed a mother. I don't need one now." She hadn't asked about Henriette and Louise-Marie. She didn't want to be our mother, she wanted a daughter to play the role that Eglantine was supposed to have played. "Why did you leave?" I asked angrily. "Why did you walk away with never another thought?"

"Your father broke his word to me. He—"

"No, why did you leave me behind?" So many years I'd waited to ask someone that question. "Why didn't you take us with you?"

Madame Latour—I couldn't think of her as Mother—sighed. "He broke his word and took you to the church to be claimed with holy water. I couldn't carry you between the worlds. Not until you were of an age to choose. I tried, don't you remember?"

I cast my mind back, searching for some memory of being carried away, but there was nothing, only emptiness. I shook my head. "Then why didn't you stay?" There must be an answer somewhere in the tangle.

"Sometimes," she said, her voice low and hollow. "Sometimes you can't save others from the beast. Sometimes you can only save yourself."

"My father was not a beast!" But I remembered what Madame Sauvin had said: *He never struck her, not really. Not what you could call a blow.* And I thought of how familiar Philippe had been in so many ways. How I'd known how to cajole him and soften his tempers. How Grace and I had made a wordless pact to protect each other, just as I'd made an unspoken promise to watch over my sisters.

But it didn't matter. I'd had a father. I'd never had the choice to have a mother. There was nothing she could do to change that now. "Goodbye, Madame Latour," I said and went into the cottage.

WHEN I ENTERED WITH my skirts full of barley and a bundle of clothing over my shoulder, Grace struggled to rise from her bed. I started towards her, but of course Eglantine was there before me. She supported Grace with an arm about her waist, helping her stand and guiding her steps slowly and stiffly to the bench by the table as I set down the bundle and poured the peas and barley into a bowl.

"I thought the curse was broken," I said.

Grace waved a hand in dismissal. "I am flesh once more, never fear. But one cannot be stone for so long without it leaving a mark."

"Can the invisible ones—" I began, then realized I hadn't seen any sign of Grace's magical servants since my return.

"They are a part of me," she said. "In time, when I'm stronger, I can conjure them again."

I thought of all the times I'd taken them for granted. The waiting at table. The music. The way they'd comforted me that night when I wept and they'd brushed my hair. And I'd thought less of it than if it had been Constance back home. I'd known it was Grace's magic, but I hadn't thought…

"Then you'll need human servants for now," I said briskly, "if you mean to stay at Bettencourt. And you'll want someone to direct them and see to stores and keep things in order." I gathered up my courage. "I…I am not accustomed to being idle. I could wish for an occupation."

Grace laughed, but it was a kindly laugh, recalling when I'd said those words before. "Sweet Alys, did you think we'd cast you out into the world?"

In my heart, I hadn't been certain. I knew who I was to Grace, and to my Lady Rose. But together they fit so closely. I hadn't known if there was a place for me.

Lady Rose…Eglantine…my sister, in a sense. The thought warmed me, but now was not the time to tell that tale. Perhaps someday soon it would no longer be painful to either of us. I was reminded of the little green-bound book still in my pocket and drew it out. Eglantine snatched it up as soon as I placed it on the table.

"*The Language of Roses*! I knew when you must have found it." No flowers fell from her mouth this time. "How lucky that it came into your hands!"

I doubted if anything partaking of mere luck had guided my path. Grace must have had the book and left it for me to find. "Was it yours, then?" I asked.

Eglantine nodded, her smile fading slightly. "Yes, a game and not a game. A way to leave a message when speech was dangerous." She pursed her lips and reached within her mouth to draw out a dark pink rosebud on a bright green stem and handed it to me. "It won't last longer than a mortal rose, I fear. The other took every scrap of my sleeping power."

Deep pink. I didn't need to thumb the pages of the book to know it stood for friendship and gratitude.

She grinned at me. "That's not all I can do. When we rebuild Bettencourt, it will be more than mere stone."

This time she spit out an acorn and, as she held it in her hand, I saw it sprout and grow, forming arches and walls until a tiny jewel of a mansion stood between her fingers. A promise of what Bettencourt could become. She closed her hand on the tiny wooden house and opened it again, revealing a cunningly carved ring of wooden keys, like the one that had opened the gates to me. "You will be welcome there."

CHAPTER THIRTY

THE LEGEND

THERE ARE STORIES OF an enchanted manor that lies in the woods. If you are fortunate, you may stumble across it on a summer's eve and see the fée at their revels. They say it is built of living wood, rising in arabesques and arches from a mossy carpet. There is nothing of stone anywhere in its walls and its garden is always full of roses, even in midwinter.

I return to visit Father and my sisters often. I arrive in a gilded palanquin carried by invisible servants. I wear a silk gown embroidered with pearls and jewels and am attended by change-lings astride pure white horses. But I never invite my family to Bettencourt. I never tell them the truth of what happened there. Father fills in the spaces with his tales. I won the love of a lord of the fée and broke the curse that bound him to a beast's shape. We were married. I am a great lady now. Father has always been free with truth for the sake of a story and he never likes to be corrected.

THE END

About the Author

Heather Rose Jones is the author of the Alpennia historic fantasy series: an alternate-Regency-era Ruritanian adventure revolving around queer women's lives, woven through with magic, alchemy, and intrigue. Her short fiction has appeared in *The Chronicles of the Holy Grail*, *Sword and Sorceress*, *Lace and Blade*, and at Podcastle.org. Heather blogs about research into lesbian-relevant motifs in history and literature at the Lesbian Historic Motif Project and has a podcast covering the field of lesbian historical fiction and historic fantasy, which includes book listings, author interviews, and short audio fiction. She lives in the San Francisco Bay Area and works as an industrial failure investigator in biotech pharmaceuticals—which has surprising parallels with writing novels. She enjoys bicycling and gardening and only reluctantly gave up a decades-long involvement in the Society for Creative Anachronism, which fed a deep love affair with the material culture of pre-modern Europe. Website: http://alpennia.com